Fear at the Fall Festival

Holly Holcraft Mysteries, Volume 2

M R Dollschnieder

Published by M R Dollschnieder, 2024.

Also by M R Dollschnieder

Holly Holcraft Mysteries
Bones in the Backyard
Fear at the Fall Festival

PROLOGUE

Perfect! Just absolutely perfect. Hands clasped in delight, the figure swathed in dark clothing, observed the scene. The light from the full moon illuminated the area just enough to see. The body sitting in the chair, the fishing rod angled just so. It was a magnificent masterpiece. After a quick glance around, the figure melted back into the darkness. Contentment filling their soul. You should always do your best, no matter the job. Mere moments after the figure was gone, a rather large fish swimming in the shallow water, found the fishing hook with the delicious worm wriggling on the end and swallowed it. Humans really shouldn't leave such delicious morsels just lying around in the water. As the fish swam off, the line hanging out of its mouth, there was a slight jerk as the body toppled over and the loosened rod drifted away until there was barely a ripple left. The magnificent masterpiece was now reduced to a piece of abstract art.

READING OF THE WILL

"And the property and all its contents are to be sold by Holly Holcraft," intoned Theodore Marlowe, probate attorney, in a dry bored voice.

"What?! You can't do that!" Bonnie Balmar screeched, her ugly face scrunched up in shock and outrage. I must admit, I felt a little satisfaction witnessing Bonnie's frustration. I know that makes me sound terrible but I recently found out that she was responsible for my husband's death and has been deliberately sabotaging my career. We are both real estate agents but any similarities end there.

We were all gathered at the lawyer's office to go over the specifics of Betty Balmar's will. She is, or rather was, Bonnie's sister. She had succumbed quite quickly to cancer recently and I still felt a pang everytime I realized I wouldn't get to speak to the cantankerous old lady anymore. I could imagine her smiling as she wrote that part of the will. She didn't much like her sister either.

We had gotten to know each other for only a short time when I sold her neighbor, Carol Oates' house and then suddenly she was gone. A large part of me felt robbed by her untimely death. Unfortunately, her sister Bonnie was still alive and well and loud. Her attitude was as loud as her garishly dyed red hair. She blamed me for her current looks but I had nothing to do with her enjoyment of food and lack of exercise. At some point we must all take responsibility for ourselves. Speaking of which, my clothes were beginning to pinch and some sort of exercise regimen definitely needed to be implemented into my future.

"I'm sorry Ms. Belmar, but I must insist that you sit down or you will be asked to leave." The lawyer's deep voice cut through the silence like a drum. Theodore Marlowe used to be a judge and brooked no nonsense from anyone. Slightly balding, tall and thin, he resembled the hanging judges from the old west. His office reflected the old west theme with pictures of cowboys herding cattle and riding horses on the walls which is probably what made me think of him that way. Law books with gold and silver stamped letters lined the bookshelves behind his large antique desk. "Your sister was quite clear on what she wanted in her will and you would do well to respect her wishes."

Bonnie's lips went in and out in frustration and she huffed a few times but finally sat down with a loud thump on her chair where she crossed her arms and glared at the lawyer. The dark furnishings in the lawyer's office, were a complement to her mood.

"With the proceeds going to the Appleby Elementary School for their reading education." He paused and looked pointedly at Bonnie over his reading glasses, in case she wanted to interrupt again, then continued. "That concludes the reading of the will. If you have any questions, you can schedule an appointment with my secretary who will also give each of you a copy." Standing up, he signaled to everyone that he was done and we should all leave.

I tried my best not to look in Bonnie's direction but failed miserably. She was still glaring at Mr. Marlowe as if she could force him to change the facts and I glanced away as she turned her head in my direction. Serves her right. You can't treat people miserably and expect to get gratitude from it.

"You knew about this. I'll get you Holly. You have no right. Don't you think you've done enough?" she growled in a deep voice as she shoved past me to exit the room. By the time I reached the door she was nowhere in sight.

"Well that was certainly interesting," said Patsy Brown, the principal of the elementary school. Patsy always looked well coiffed and had a predilection for designer clothes. I don't know how she did it with all those children constantly around her. "Congratulations on selling the home. I know the families are all going to be grateful for the funds, especially the librarian. She's had to make do with so little for such a long time."

"Yes, it will certainly make a difference to the kids," I replied. As a tourist destination in the mountains, our district didn't have the greatest literacy rates, what with people always moving in and then leaving again.

"I only wonder why she did it," she continued glancing around and lowering her voice. "She had quite the reputation for being cranky."

I smiled, my eyes beginning to water. "Yes, she did."

"You know, you should come to the PTA meeting tonight. You could let everyone know about this incredible donation and we'll be discussing plans for the Annual Fall Festival. Might be a great way to pick up some new clients." She patted my shoulder as she walked past me to the door.

As Patsy walked away, it did make me wonder, why was there no mention of her books? Betty had told me she was the author of the popular spicy series of romance books under the pen name Ophelia Love. There had to have been quite the income from that. Well, it wasn't my place to say anything. If it was to be a secret, I certainly wouldn't be the one to reveal it.

"Oh, Miss Holcraft," called out Mr. Marlowe, still standing behind his desk. "Would you hold up a moment?" I turned around and headed back to his desk. "I have one more thing for you. You'll understand why I didn't want to give it to you in front of Miss Belmar." He gave an apologetic smile and handed me a small manila envelope.

"Why thank you Mr. Marlowe and I do understand," I answered, returning his smile and feeling like the Cheshire cat.

A MEETING WITH ALMA

Stepping outside was quite the contrast from the dark paneled office with its stale air. It was a beautiful autumn day here in Appleby, a small town in the mountains. The sun was warm but the air was brisk, perfect for a cup of hot apple cider before a crackling fire. Before that happened though, I would need to call Mr. Marlowe's secretary and make an appointment to get the listing agreement signed so I could put it on the multiple listing service. I would also need to schedule appointments for pictures and video and perhaps have the home inspector come by to take a look just in case there were any issues with the home. It's always better to have things fixed beforehand if possible.

I also had to hurry to my next appointment with Alma Hotchkiss. She was selling her million dollar home and I had already missed two appointments with her, through no fault of my own, and I could hardly be late this time after she had granted me the listing. Turns out she is also a dog lover, and a chance encounter by the lake with a stranger's dog gave me the in I needed.

After settling into my car, I opened the package. Inside was just an old bronze key with gold floral flourishes on a gold chain, no note, leaving me to wonder what Betty had been up to. I slipped it on over my neck as a way to keep Betty close. double checked my bag to make sure my listing agreement and purchase agreement paperwork were still safely tucked inside. Not only did I get to list the house, but Mrs. Hotchkiss already had a buyer. Of course, this double luck made me wonder what was going to go wrong. I mean, doesn't something always go wrong when things seem to be going too well? I put my phone on 'do not disturb' and shifted my car into drive. Nothing was going to interfere with this meeting.

The Hotchkiss house was halfway up the mountain in the luxury homes area to the north west of the town. The drive over was peaceful and quiet. Pine trees were dominant in the landscape with just a few deciduous trees remaining that were losing their leaves. It was really nice to have some green year round. When the first snows came in November it would really look beautiful with the snow piled on the branches. Even trees with no leaves looked pretty with snow on them.

I pulled up to the two story, 1920s home and gave it an appraising look. I suspected the house also had a basement, technically making the home three stories which would increase its value significantly. Of course with a buyer in tow, they had probably already decided on a price. Stepping onto the spacious covered porch I banged the metal bear door knocker a few times. Mrs. Hotchkiss herself answered the door at my knock. She was a trim woman in her late 60s but looked much younger.

"Oh great," Mrs. Hotchkiss looked over my shoulder to the driveway as another car pulled in. "My buyer is here also." Turning to look in the same direction, my eyebrows rose to my hairline when I saw who the buyer was. Exiting the car, Emmeline Davis, a slight girl in her twenties, twisted her fingers together nervously when she saw it was me.

"Is something wrong?" Mrs. Hotchkiss inquired as Emmeline joined us on the porch. Putting on a smile, although I was feeling entirely the opposite, I answered. "Not at all Mrs. Hotchkiss. It's just that I've been showing Emmeline houses lately."

"Oh dear, and do call me Alma. Is this true Emmeline?"

Emmeline tilted her head to the side like a bird and then shrugged. "Yes? I'm sorry. I couldn't find a house I liked and when I saw the pictures of this one, I convinced daddy that it would be a good investment and he agreed. I feel just awful Holly, not calling you, but I was so embarrassed that I couldn't find one I liked and I thought you would be mad at me." She put her hands behind her back and looked at the ground.

Emmeline was what you would call a daddy's girl as she had him firmly twisted around her finger. I should be mad at her for not calling me but that never earns you repeat business. I could see that in a few years she would grow into her awkwardness and become a really beautiful woman. I only hoped she learned some real life values before then.

Of course I would never tell her this because I'm a professional peacemaker, so instead I said, "I would never be mad at you Emmeline. It's my job to show you as many houses as you need to decide." It didn't matter if that was three dozen and counting.

"Well, now that that's settled, come inside. It's a bit chilly out and I had the cook make us lunch," said Alma, ushering us in and closing the door. The smell of freshly baked bread made my mouth water.

Now that I was inside, I looked admiringly at the decorative ceilings and elaborate ornamentation. The house was immaculate. High ceilings dominated the space and the view over the mountainside was spectacular with downtown Appleby appearing in the distance. Alma gave us the official tour of the house before lunch, highlighting the features of the 1920s art deco house.

"You should be an agent yourself, you do such an excellent job explaining," I said after the tour. "Your house is absolutely amazing."

"Thank you for the compliment. My father was in real estate and I suppose I've picked up some of his mannerisms." She looked around at the living room with the cathedral ceilings. "I plan on decorating the house in the 1920s style for the annual Christmas Tour of Homes since it will be our last year."

I looked at her puzzled. "Won't Emmeline be living here then?"

Alma gave a radiant smile. "Yes, she will, but we've made an agreement that Albert and I can come back for the holidays." She gave

Emmeline a big hug, "It's going to be so great. Emmeline's parents and I have known each other for years." Emmeline gave a little half hearted smile. I had the feeling the decision hadn't been hers.

"Ma'am, lunch is ready," announced the cook, a plump woman wearing an apron dusted with speckles of flour. In my mind, that meant she must be really good. Speckles of flour is always a good indicator of homemade to me, mainly because I never use it.

"Great," said Alma. "Let's go eat and deal with the paperwork after."

My suspicion about the cook had been correct. We dined on a delicious bouillabaisse accompanied by homemade crusty bread with butter. Alma signed the listing agreement and they both signed the purchase agreement. I would need to docusign them to her husband Albert who was out of town but they were as good as done.

SEVERAL HOURS AND A full belly later, I met up with Omar Marroquin, he's a co-worker at my office and had asked me for some help with his business. I thought he was just a flirt but I had misjudged him and he just needed some help. I met him in his office because I still think he's kind of a snoop. I sat across the desk from him and looked at his computer screen which was displaying pictures of his current listing. Clutter could be seen in most of the photos.

"You really do need to get some better pictures, Omar. Take some baskets over to the house and fill them with everything on the counters and then you can put it all back after the pictures are taken. This gives a clean picture so buyers can imagine their own stuff in the area," I advised.

"I never thought of that," he said. "Real estate is so much more difficult than they tell you in the classes."

I laughed. "The joke is that the classes only get you ready for the test. The actual work is a whole different ball game. You know you can't only do real estate stuff and expect to meet clients, you really need to think outside the box. Volunteer in the community. The fall festival is coming up soon and then we'll have the snow bunnies show up. Maybe check out advertising at the ski slopes." Omar was middle-aged and good looking. I was actually surprised that he wasn't doing better for himself. He would look great in print ads.

"Thanks Holly, I really appreciate this. I feel like if I can just get a couple things going I'll be good. Hey, how's your car running? Do you need me to take a look at it?" He reached out to touch my hand and I pulled it away.

My car needed a new battery recently and then right after it was installed it wouldn't start. "It's running great. The battery cable was just loose. Once I tightened that up it ran great."

Omar looked like he didn't believe me. "You tightened it up?"

"Okay, Travis checked it for me." I admitted.

"The cop?"

"Yeah that's him. Actually he's a detective."

Omar fiddled with his papers. "Are you seeing him?"

I mentally threw my hands in the air. "Why does everyone keep asking me that? I just met him during the investigation." Suddenly I wanted to be anywhere but here. "I think you should be good for now. If you just get some new pictures, I'm sure that listing will get a bunch of offers." I stood up to leave, "Let me know how it goes. I really do have to run now. Good luck."

I smiled while I made my goodbyes and then walked across the building to Vana Dago's office. I told myself it was just to visit her but partly I wanted to ensure Omar didn't come to my office for 'just one more thing'. Vana was my co-worker and close friend. She was like the sister I always wanted but never knew I needed.

"Hey Vana how's it going?" I plopped into the chair in front of her desk where she was sitting typing away on her computer, a bag of pretzels open next to her. "Rough day?" She pushed the pretzels my way and I grabbed a few.

"I just met with Omar to go over his business," I said, frowning and popping a pretzel in my mouth. Saltiness flooded over my tongue.

"You don't look too happy about it."

"I don't, he's just," I grimaced, not having the words to clarify my thoughts. As she opened her mouth I cut in myself. "I know. I know. I need to stop being so nice."

"You know, he's been doing real estate for nearly a year. He should have it figured out by now." Vana was always succinct and had a low tolerance for nonsense, unlike me. People pleasing is in my DNA. I suppose it comes from my parents fighting all the time. Thankfully, they are now divorced.

I shrugged. "You know how it goes. When things get a little tough, people falter. Thanks for the pretzels," I said snagging a few more before returning to my own office. Settling behind my desk, her comment about Omar made me curious. I navigated to the Department of Real Estate website and looked up Omar's license.

That's interesting. This wasn't Omar's first time as a licensed agent. He'd held a license in another state five years ago but had become relicensed just nine months ago. Maybe he couldn't cut it the first time but wanted to try again. I'd have to ask him about it. Right now I need to get my work done and get ready for the parent teacher meeting tonight. It was high time I became involved in the community again and the decision actually made me feel good. It felt right to branch out into something new.

The murders the previous month hadn't done much to help with my general feeling of malaise lately. Maybe it was just menopause or middle age. Maybe I just needed some more sunshine. I made a mental note to spend more time outside.

I left a note for my assistant, Joe Marvel, to set up appointments with Mr. Marlowe's secretary to get the listing agreement on Betty's house signed and to arrange for a home inspection and pictures and video. I also left the completed listing and purchase agreements for the Hotchkiss deal with instructions for him to send them to Albert Hotchkiss for electronic signature.

There is nothing like a great assistant. Joe had only been with me for half a year but I don't know how I got anything done before I hired him. We'd had a bit of a fuss last month where I fired him and then rehired him but now he was back to his usual excellent self. With that all taken care of, I left for home for a quick bite to eat and to give my dog some dinner.

PTA MEETING

My house was a short twenty minute drive up in the mountains. The beauty of the scenery always helped to relax me and put me in a good mood. I can't imagine how people who live in the city all the time do it without all of the nature that encompasses me on a daily basis. The winding two lane road cuts through the shadowy forest of pine trees. Pine needles cover the hillsides and occasionally I even see a deer or racoon wandering through.

As I dropped my keys on the stand by the front door, I heard the click-click of the doggy door as Ginger came through the kitchen into the living room to greet with me with a woof and her tail wagging a mile a minute.

"Hello Ginger, did you miss me?" I gave her a good back and ear scratching and then topped off her water and kibble dishes whereupon she sat in front of her one empty dish and watched me as I made myself a sandwich. "I know Ginger it's coming. Mommy won't forget your real dinner." Besides, it's not as if she would let me forget she had canned food coming. She never does. Her dinner was gone in exactly 30 seconds. My sandwich, chips and diet coke, took a bit longer to finish.

I adopted Ginger as a pup shortly after I lost my husband. There's nothing worse than coming home to an empty house. I used to have a cat but she was also lost in the accident. I figured a dog would distract me from what I was missing and Ginger did all that and more. She might be ten years old but she was as spry as ever. They say big dogs don't live as long, but Ginger wasn't showing any signs of slowing down.

Ginger whined as I picked up my keys and coat. "Sorry girl, I've got a meeting tonight but it won't be very long and then we can both watch tv together and have some ice cream. Okay?" She cocked her head to the side and then went to lie down on the couch. Sometimes I think she really does understand me.

"Good girl Ginger, mommy won't be long. Keep the house safe. Make good choices." Locking the door behind me, I was grateful for such a wonderful dog. With a 70 pound Doberman-Shepherd mix inside, I don't have to worry about anyone breaking in.

TONIGHT WAS GOING TO be my first PTA meeting in a very long while, not that I had any young children anymore, just my granddaughter, but it did seem the school district was always short on volunteers and it could be a great way to help out my granddaughter and if I gathered some real estate listings on the way, that would be a bonus. I had been very involved in the PTA in my previous town, when my daughter was young and, if I was going to be honest, part of me also missed it. I had three really close friends here, but it wasn't the same as mixing with members of a large group. There's a certain camaraderie in being a part of something bigger than yourself.

The meeting was held in the high school gym, since it was the biggest space in town. The bleachers were all pulled out on one side and the mayor stood at a podium in the center of the basketball court. Since our school district was so small, the parent-teacher association had decided to represent all the grades, K-12th. That way they could support all the kids and parents wouldn't have to deal with multiple fundraisers. Most of the fundraisers ended up being community events anyway and the next one up was the aforementioned Fall Festival.

I figured I would start out with something small, just a member of a committee or two. Maybe it was finding out the truth about my husband's death, that Bonnie was the drunk driver that caused his accident, but I felt free and a need to belong somewhere, not that I didn't before but my recent experiences had shown me that it was way past time for me to be 'home.'

Every year the festival was held on the east end of the lake, which typically froze around this time and we would have ice skating, games, food booths and baking contests. Maybe I could enter the baking contest. It would encourage me to step up my game and actually learn how to bake.

Mayor Peter Townsend, dressed in a tailored gray suit, tapped lightly on the microphone to direct the attention his way. He was one of those stately men who always seemed to have a smile on his face. I guess you need that in politics. After the customary greetings, he dug into the point of the meeting.

His pleasant baritone voice filled the air as he spoke. "The City Council partners with our local PTA every year to put on the annual Fall Festival with proceeds divided between the council's charity groups and the schools. This year I'm delighted that we have a new volunteer to lead the event. She's a local real estate agent and a great asset to our community."

My ears perked up at the mention of 'real estate agent." If it's Bonnie, I'll have to resign before I even start. There's no way I'll ever work under her direction. But what's the chances of that? There's quite a few agents in our small town. The next words really made me sit up and take notice.

"Let's all give a warm welcome to Holly Holcraft. Holly, would you please stand so we can all see who you are? Holly recently helped solve the murder of our dear Amos Belroy and I know we are all looking forward to working with her."

Wait. what? As everyone began clapping, I slowly stood to my feet and plastered a surprised smile on my face. This was not what I had in mind when I decided to volunteer. "Thank you Mayor Townsend," I nodded in his direction as I sat back down. Now was not the time to correct him. I would promptly resign as soon as the meeting was over.

The rest of the meeting was filled with the listing of committees that needed volunteers and the notice that sign up sheets were located on the other side of the court on long tables for people to choose from. As the meeting ended I was suddenly surrounded by all ages of women, someone grabbed my elbow and whispered in my ear. "Holly, I volunteered you. I knew you would be just wonderful for this." Turning to face the culprit, my admonition faded as I saw it was Alma Hotchkiss with a huge beaming smile on her face. Who was I to take that away? Plus what could I do? She was one of the most influential people in town and obviously had the Mayor's ear. I finally managed to stammer out, "thanks. I'll try to do my best."

She side hugged me as she said, "I know you will."

"I do have a question, what happened to the previous chair?"

Alma made a slight frown and looked apologetic, "He's not able to do it this year. "It's okay, He has all of the groundwork done, contacts and so forth. The ladies will help you," she added brightly before rushing off.

Other voices started kicking in. Over the jumble, a phrase caught my ear. "Wait. The Blume house? Isn't this held at the lake every year?" I asked.

"Well usually it is," a middle aged blonde woman said sadly. "But since they found the body in the lake, it was decided to move it."

"The body in the lake?" I said, my eyes springing wide open.

"Yes, it's quite sad really, it seems he had gone ice fishing and froze to death, possibly after he fell asleep."

I frowned, "Fell asleep while fishing? How old was this person?"

"84 next month."

"84!?"

This was puzzling but I decided to let it go, I mean, some 80 year olds are quite spry, still it didn't seem right.

"Alright. Well, will I be able to speak with Pete if I run into problems? Maybe get some advice on the direction to go?"

It was suddenly silent and all of the ladies' eyes dropped to the floor. Several of them twisting their lips but not speaking. Finally, a voice said quietly, "Pete's the one in the lake."

My eyebrows rose to my hairline. "The chairman of the Festival?" My voice came out in a squeak while my brain tried to process the information.

"One and the same," said another voice.

I suppressed an urge to scream and clenched my fists at my sides, "you could have led with that. Let me get this straight. I'm the chair of the fall festival that now has to be moved because the predecessor died ice fishing in our one and only lake that usually hosts the festival?" The ladies all nodded. "And now it is going to be held at the Blume...wait, isn't that the haunted house?" My eyes went wide. No way, I'm going in a spooky house at Halloween time. I looked around desperately for Alma so I could back out of this but the little tart was gone.

"It's almost Halloween and a full moon is coming up. That will really bring the crazies out so make sure you have strong security," said another woman. The ladies' voices began again and I held my hands up for silence.

"I need a moment to think on this. Why don't we meet in the conference room at my office, Front Door Realty, tomorrow afternoon to go over the plans?" Heads began nodding in affirmation and a few voices said, "yes, sounds good."

With plans made to meet the next day, I drove home muttering to myself the whole way, "I am not getting involved in another death. I simply am not. What kind of old man goes ice fishing and falls asleep in the freezing cold? How would he fall out of his chair into the water? Was he in a chair? I would be in a chair. No, no, no. Stop it Holly." I drove home completely oblivious to the beautiful fall foliage.

BERNARD

Totally stressed out as I pulled into my garage, I resolved to take Ginger for a walk. She had been cooped up all day and she would protect me against any varmints in the woods. I fed her dinner, which was gone in exactly 30 seconds, stepped on the trash can lever to open the lid and remembered, I had already fed her dinner before I left as I saw the empty can in the trash. Ugh. "I guess you got two dinners tonight huh? You couldn't have let me know before I fed you again?" An innocent look from those beautiful brown eyes, was all I got in return.

Shrugging, I tossed the second can in and then grabbed her leash and put both of our jackets on. There is nothing like a crisp autumn evening in the woods to clear your mind. The pine trees are magnificent whether it's day or night and the woods smell so good. Sure there's only random street lights and it's rather dark and you can hear mystery noises, but they're my mystery noises and I find them comforting, little raccoon families ambling around collecting food, the occasional howl from a wolf, comforting.

Ginger's ears perked up at a sound from up ahead. She is big so I wasn't too worried. Then I heard a trash can fall over and something came running towards me. "It's okay Ginger. It's probably just a raccoon," I said to calm her except this something came running straight at me and jumped up on me.

"Holly, I'm so sorry," came a gentleman's deep voice out of the dark. "Bernard, get down," he commanded.

Bernard? The name seemed familiar to me and the dog evidently knew me. Then it came to me. "Oh, you're the man from the dog park. Thank you for letting me use him. Do you live around here?"

"Oh yes, my house is just around the bend, but it's back a bit so you don't really see it." He extended his hand to me in the light of the flashlight he carried. "I'm Ben Brown and I'm the butler extraordinaire at the Hotchkiss house." I could almost hear the humor in his voice as he spoke.

I shook the proffered hand. "You're the...but I didn't see you when I was there the other day?" I replied confused.

"You wouldn't have. My son and daughter-in-law just had their first child, my granddaughter. I've been helping them out. It's kind of my thing," he laughed at the joke.

"So you know, Alma is letting me sell her house. Thank you for that. I guess Bonnie didn't work out."

"Hmm, such a shame some complaints about her came to Mrs. Hotchkiss's attention. What she did to you was absolutely reprehensible."

Now I felt terrible. How did I not know my neighbor? "I'm really sorry, we haven't met before," I began but he cut me off politely.

"Now, don't you worry about that. I spend most of my time at the Hotchkiss place and am rarely here."Bernard here is my son's dog. I only have him until the baby comes home. She came early, you know."

"Oh, I am so sorry. If I can do anything to help, let me know. This is Ginger," I said pointing to my dog.

A big smile creased his face. "Oh, we are very familiar with Ginger. She comes to visit when you leave for work."

Shock battled with anger at this news. "She what? How does she get out of the yard?" I looked crossly at my dog who put up her ears and cocked her head innocently. "She's always home when I get back."

"She probably jumps over the fence and then jumps back in. Sorry Ginger, I didn't mean to get you in trouble," he directed to the dog. I

was beginning to like this guy. "I can help you fix it so she can't get out."
Ginger looked at Ben at this news with dismay and gave an anxious
whine which was not lost on me.

"This is for your own safety," I admonished her. "What if you
encountered a bear? Well, we really should be getting on, but thank
you again for all your help and let me know what I can do about the
fence. Goodbye Bernard." I added, giving the shaggy dog a little scratch
behind the ears.

"Oh Holly," Ben called after me. "You might want to say hello to
Mildred, she lives just past my house now, around the bend."

"The candy store owner?"

"Yes, one and the same. She just moved back this past weekend.
She'd been renting it out you know."

"No, I didn't know. But thank you Ben, I'll be sure to do that." Yet
another neighbor had moved on and I didn't even meet them. What
kind of an agent am I that I do door knocking everywhere but around
my own house? I made a vow to do a future party and invite all my
neighbors over. Ben and Bernard vanished back into the darkness, the
sound of their footsteps fading away.

I walked around the bend, past what I now knew was Ben's house,
and beyond to Mildred's. Her front yard was a profusion of flowers. I
could see them all quite well because I unfortunately set off her security
light.

The screen door creaked as she came to peer out. "Good evening
Mildred. It's me, Holly. Ben just told me you moved back in."

"Oh, hello Holly. Yes, such a delightful man. I'm so happy to be
back in my own home again."

"Ben said you were renting it out?"

"Oh yes, once my husband passed it was difficult. Memories you
know. So I rented an apartment in town but I'm tired of the town life
and I miss my garden. So here I am." She ended on a jolly note.

"I'm glad you're my neighbor. If you need help with anything, I have become quite proficient at finding handymen with my phone." We both laughed at the joke.

Mildred shivered in the damp air, "I should be getting back in but come by sometime for coffee and I'm sure there's some dog biscuits around." Ginger whined and wagged her tail at the word.

"I sure will Mildred. Have a nice night." The trip back home was less eventful and Ginger and I had a most peaceful evening.

OFFICE WORK

Morning sunbeams danced across my bedroom floor as I readied for work. After the crisis of a few weeks ago, when I solved two murders and prevented a third, I had buckled down on my work. With the double commission from the Hotchkiss/Emmeline sale, I will be sitting pretty as far as my bills go and with money in the bank to pay my taxes. Take that Bonnie! Being financially secure, however temporary it may be, is a wonderful feeling. Of course it comes with the caveat that nothing in real estate is a done deal until title is filed.

My assistant Joe was supervising a home inspection at one of my listings. He turned out to be really amazing at inspections and although there was still a bit of a trust issue, I couldn't deny that he did excellent work when he wanted to.

My drive into town was uneventful and the bright sunlight on the lake sent shimmering sparkles across the water.

I was sitting at my desk, looking up properties on my computer when my phone rang and I looked at it to see that it was the owner of said listing, Daniel McCready. In his 60s and newly retired, he had discovered that he did not like mountain living. I'm going to say it was because of the several feet of snow every year.

"Hello Daniel, how's the inspection going?"

His gruff voice came back over the line, "It's fine. Look, the appraisal came in my email this morning and it says the value of my house is only $400,000. Can you do something about that?" I cringed at his words. I was afraid this was going to happen. Despite my best advice, Daniel had accepted an offer at $40,000 over the list price but no lender will finance over the appraised value so that extra $40k was meaningless but to him it was dollar signs dancing in his eyes.

"I'm sorry, the house only appraised at $400,000, which as you know, is what I told you the price would most likely be."

He took advantage of my pause to whine, "but that's not enough money." Taking a deep breath, I prepared to do battle. Politely. Because he's my client. I reminded myself mentally of this three times before responding.

"The banks only lend up to the value of the property. I explained this to you." I had, multiple times.

"But they offered $40,000 over the asking price. Can't we take one of the other offers?"

"Daniel, I told you this could happen and you agreed with it. We can cancel but we'll have to start all the timelines over again, so you're looking at another 30-45 days or more and you said you didn't want to have to spend another winter shoveling snow. Even if the other buyers are still available and willing, escrow won't close before the snows come and you might be stuck with moving in the snow. Would you even want to take that risk?"

Silence came from the other end for so long I began to think the call had dropped.

"I think I might," he said slowly.

Grrr. "Okay, I might have a solution. I can take one percent off my commission. That will put a little more back in your pocket. But that's all I can do." Here I go, giving in again. The girls will kill me. But a closed sale is better than no sale. Right?

"Okay. I'll sell it to these guys." A deep sigh came over the line. "But I'm not happy." *Neither am I Daniel, neither am I.*

What can I say? It's people like Daniel that put joy into my job; when their escrow closes and they move away. I punched in Joe's number to check up on the home inspection.

"Hey Joe, how's the inspection going?"

"Great. Nothing out of the ordinary. Mr. McCready's a bit grumpy."

I laughed. "Yes, he is. I have a meeting in a few minutes, did you get my notes regarding Betty's house and the Hotchkiss contracts?"

"Yup, already filed and sent. Dottie, Mr. Marlowe's secretary said you could just drop off the contracts and she'll get them signed and send them back."

"Great. Thank you Joe. I put a lockbox on the side gate. Just send the photographer a code to access it." That reminds me, I need to call a company to do the estate sale and perhaps I should drop by and let the buyer's of Carol's home next door know Betty's would be available soon, in case they know anyone wanting to buy.

"Sure thing. I should be done here soon."

"Awesome, you are wonderful." Disconnecting the call, I saw that it was time for the Fall Festival meeting. "Just great," I muttered, shaking my head. I closed my eyes and took a few deep breaths to center myself, grabbed some scratch paper, pens and business cards, then made my way to the conference room to find out what kind of mayhem a few ladies could cause. This was going to be fun. Right?

I ran into Omar right outside my door. "Holly. I changed those pictures like you said and I've already got several showings set up. Thanks for your help. How about I take you out to lunch to celebrate?"

"Oh, I'm so sorry, Omar. I've a meeting right now and several fires to put out. Besides, you should probably wait to celebrate until you've got an offer." I gave him my mom smile. "I've really got to run now, but that's great news and I'm glad it helped." Before he could say another word I hurriedly walked away.

THE VOLUNTEERS ONLY filled a small portion of the conference room which was usually used for home buying presentations and such. A whiteboard sat on the wall at the front and rows of chairs lined the room. The ladies had taken it upon themselves to liberate the first two rows of chairs and had formed them into a circle. They all took a seat as I entered the room.

The blonde woman from the mayor's meeting handed me several sheets of paper. "These are the committee sign ups. The chairman of each is listed on the top."

"Thank you," I said, taking them from her and flipping through them as I addressed the group. Hey, I'm a professional multi-tasker, what can I say? "Why don't we all say our names and what position we are handling?" I looked around the circle of women expectantly.

A short blonde woman with curly hair stood up. "My name is Cindy and I'll be handling the bake sale. Will you be bringing any baked goods? Pete always made us several dozen cookies."

That was a surprise, Pete baked? "I'm afraid I haven't baked in a long time, unless you count prepackaged cookie dough." The shock on the ladies' faces was paramount.

"Hmm. Do you have any hobbies?" she asked not to be daunted.

I shook my head, "sadly no."

"Nothing? Not even gardening or crafting?"

"I'm afraid not. My only hobbies are drinking wine and selling houses." The ladies looked less than impressed. "I am good at organizing, which I'm sure is why Alma," I paused, not wanting to throw her under the bus. Was she not supposed to volunteer me? "Thought I would be perfect for the job," I finished with a smile. The ladies seemed to brighten at this prospect.

"Well then, let's move on," I said. After all the introductions, we moved on to planning events. "I would like all of you to tell me how you plan on handling your events and any ideas you might have for the group."

"Oh," said Louella, an older woman with her hand over her mouth. "That's not how Pete did it." Brown, blonde and gray heads shook back and forth. Mentally rolling my eyes, I asked the dreaded question.

"Okay then, how did Pete do it?" I wanted to mention Pete was now dead but thought better of it.

A short stocky woman with her hair in a light brown bob raised her hand hesitantly and I nodded in her direction. "Hi. Patty here. Pete just gave us a list of things he needed done and then we did them. He uh, he didn't ever want our advice," she said as she sat back down.

I pressed my hands together and bounced them on my chin. I could see this was going to be one of those, 'we've always done it this way' crowds and I was going to have to head them off or be stuck with 'but Pete' forever.

I struck a sympathetic pose and spoke softly. "Unfortunately, Pete is no longer with us and his usual site is no longer available. I'm going to need all of you ladies to work with me here. We have a new venue with new logistics and I really need all of you to step up to the plate. After all this is for the children. So any ideas that you have, I am more than welcome to listen to them. We're in this together ladies," I ended on a positive note.

The ladies' faces all brightened. Maybe I was wrong and they weren't a 'we always do it this way' crowd. Maybe they just needed an opportunity to shine. It was amazing what could be accomplished when you recognized a person's worth. After that I was assailed with numerous wonderful ideas and the ladies all left the meeting with excitement leaving me with a smile on my face.

ENCOURAGEMENT

"You're sure happy." I turned to see Vana behind me as I walked back to my office.

"Yes, the meeting went very well."

"What meeting? Did I miss something?"

"You are looking at the new chairman for the town's Fall Festival," I said proudly.

"Wow," she exclaimed. "Look at you getting all civic minded. I knew it would happen eventually."

"Yeah, well, Alma Hotchkiss volunteered me for it. How could I refuse?"

Vana pursed her lips, then shrugged her shoulders. "Hopefully it will pay off. The referrals from her will be awesome." She pressed her lips together trying not to laugh. I narrowed my eyes at her suspiciously.

"What?"

"I was just going to say that they will pay off as long as you don't let any more dogs push you in the mud," she said laughing.

"Very funny," I retorted back. "But she did ask if I would be present at the inspections. Which I will be since there are no murders to solve. I hardly think anyone is going to knock off Alma." Reaching my office door, I unlocked it and led Vana inside.

"Speaking of murders, have you talked to Travis?" At my hesitation she continued. "It's not his fault, you know. He did try to tell you. Don't be like those movies where you miss out on love over something stupid."

Taking a deep breath, I blew it out slowly, giving myself a moment to think. "I just don't think I'm ready. I would feel like I've betrayed my husband somehow."

Vana put her arm around my shoulders and squeezed. "You couldn't possibly have known any of this was going to happen," she said comfortingly.

"That's just it," I cried, dropping my notes on the desk. "Shouldn't I have? Why did I never look into his death further? Why did I just accept he was gone?" I paced the small room, clenching my hands into fists. "I'll admit, Travis is attractive and nice and polite and everything I would want. But I just feel this guilt." I couldn't explain it to her. She was my dearest friend, but I couldn't put into words this feeling that I had let him down; had let my daughter, Penelope down. "I just can't," I said quietly. "It's better to just leave it be."

"Well," Vana said brightly. "If it's gonna happen. It will happen."

Joe entering the office thankfully put an end to the conversation. "Hi Holly. Thanks again for giving me back my job. I won't let you down." I had fired Joe for colluding with Bonnie Belmar, my nemesis, and then rehired him after having a talk with his sister. After she locked us in her escape room, but that's another story.

"You don't have to keep thanking me. You're a great assistant," I smiled warmly at him.

"I got your email to change your commission on the McCready house. Do I need to adjust the price also?" Uh oh.

Vana raised her eyebrows at me. "What's this? Are you increasing your commission?"

I shifted uncomfortably. "Yes, please Joe. The appraisal came in low." He looked back and forth between the two of us and wisely chose to work at one of the outside cubicles.

"I'll just get started on this out here," he said as he walked through the door, closing it behind him. I could see him settling into the desk across from my office through the glass door.

I smiled at Vana as I sat in my desk chair. "Daniel was going to cancel the transaction because the appraisal came in too low."

"So you caved and offered to cut your commission." Vana stated it matter of factly. "You're never going to be able to retire if you keep doing this."

"I know. I know you're right, but I can't help it if I want to help people. Is that so wrong?"

"It is if it takes money out of your pocket. How are you going to pay your taxes if you can barely keep your head above water? And now that you know Bonnie hates you, she's going to try even harder to screw with you. Do you want to make her happy?"

I twisted my lips as I whispered, "no."

Vana sighed as she dropped onto the couch. "I'm afraid she's going to start messing with me now, because we're friends."

I looked at her in shock. "Oh, no. Has she done something?"

"No. I just have a feeling. What are we going to do?"

"You're asking me?" I said, raising my eyebrows. "Now we really are in trouble," I chided her as my phone buzzed.

"Holly. You've got to get down here," came a whispered voice over the line. "It's me, Mildred from the candy store. There's some guy here trying to swindle Louella out of her house." Before I could answer, she had hung up the phone.

Her words got my goat up. Is that the correct phrase? I just hate it when people try to take advantage of senior citizens. I grabbed my jacket off the hook by the door and put it on. "I've got to run Vana. Mildred says someone's trying to take advantage of Louella. Do you want to come?"

She shook her head. "Can't I've got a client coming in. Let me know how it goes though."

"Sure thing," I said as I hurried out the door.

IN A PICKLE

The candy shop was only three doors down from the office. Not a good thing if you've got a sweet tooth. Let's just say, Mildred gets a lot of business from my office.

The bell above the door tinkled as I opened it. Stepping through, I saw Mildred behind the counter beckoning to me. She was standing next to a young, thin woman with perfectly styled brunette hair and dressed in the cutest baby blue designer sweater which went great with her green eyes.

"Hi Holly. It's so good of you to drop in." She said it loudly, but then dropped her voice to whisper. "That guy is trying to get Louella to sign up for a reverse mortgage but I've heard what he's saying and it's not right. You've got to do something."

Mildred had been running the candy shop alone, ever since her husband passed. She was your typical, white-haired, plump grandmotherly type who was loved by everyone and when she said to do something, you did it. She looked out for everyone and everyone looked out for her.

I took a few minutes to listen to the man by pretending to peruse the floor to ceiling shelves filled with every candy you could imagine. It was like walking into Wonka's shop. I can't even begin to describe the wonderful scents that filled the air. Behind the counter, she had a small ice cream set up for shakes and sundaes.

"Have you got any black licorice?" I asked aloud while looking at some animal shaped marshmallow pops. My granddaughter Chloe would love those.

"Right over here," beckoned Mildred indicating a location right next to Louella's table with nary a piece of black licorice in sight. Did I mention, she's also very smart?

"If you'll just sign right here, then you'll be able to start getting money next month." The man with the slick voice was dressed for the part with a dashing suit and tie. His hair looked like he spent hours in front of the bathroom mirror getting it just right.

Louella sounded unsure as she asked, "This won't affect my equity?"

"Not at all, that money will still be there for you. Just sign right here." The pushy man indicated a line at the bottom of the document. I turned around and met Louella's eyes. She looked relieved to see me.

"Hi," I said, extending my hand. "I'm Holly and I'm Louella's real estate agent. If you don't mind, I'd like to take a look at that document." I whisked the paperwork off the tabletop before he had a chance to answer. His smile changed to a frown.

Scanning through the pages, I saw that she would be giving up title to her house to the stranger.

"Hey! Give that to me," the man said angrily as he attempted to grab it from me, but I turned and he met my shoulder instead.

"I'm sorry, sir, but I don't think Louella will be signing this today." I turned to look at him, while shifting the paper behind my back. He stood there huffing and angry, his hands clenched into fists at his side.

"I need that back. That's my paperwork," he growled as he reached around me and snatched the papers back. I stepped back suddenly.

"Did you just assault me? Did you ladies see that?" I questioned my eyes wide "I think he just assaulted me." The almost thief licked his lips nervously as he looked around at each of us. He gave a smile as he backed towards the door. "Nice meeting you ladies. I'll just be going now." He must have jumped three feet in the air when Detective Travis Smart tapped him on the shoulder. "Is there a problem here?" The baritone voice caused my heart to beat faster. The thief whirled around and raised his hands in the air.

"I called Travis, when I called you," explained a smiling Mildred. "He's working in town you know," she added with a wink in my direction. I hadn't known.

"Look, if you guys don't mind, I'm just gonna go," said the thief.

"Actually, I do mind," said Travis, reaching forward and snagging the papers. "What are these?"

"Officer Smart, this man just attempted to swindle Louella here, out of her house. Those are the papers to prove it," I said. The thief wavered between grabbing the papers from Travis or lunging for the door. His hesitation cost him dearly as Louella swung her handbag at his head. As he ducked, Mildred grabbed his arm, spinning the man around and pinning him against a table top with his hand behind his back.

"Don't all of you just stand there gawping at me. Come give me a hand," she exclaimed.

While we all stood in shock, Travis pulled out his handcuffs and arrested the man. As he left out the door with the thief and placed him in the back of his car, we finally found our voices.

"Wow, Mildred, I had no idea you could do that," I marveled at her.

"Oh, it's nothing. I've been taking some karate classes over in Morecroft since my husband passed. You ladies should come join me. There's one tonight. You never know when it might come in handy."

Louella looked doubtful. "I don't know about that. At my age, I might strain something important." Mildred cocked an eyebrow at her. They were the same age but where Mildred was plump, Louella was as skinny as a rail.

I stifled a laugh. "I just might take you up on that. I could use some exercise."

"Who was that dreamy guy?" asked the new woman.

Mildred snapped her fingers. "Oh, I almost forgot. Let me introduce you to Meredith Maroney. I met her at a writers convention in Morecroft. She's a sleuth also," she added proudly.

"I am not a sleuth." I muttered as I shook my head at Mildred.

"You solved Amos's murder and saved Jerry. That makes you a sleuth in my book," she insisted stubbornly. "That dreamy guy is Travis

Smart. He's a detective from Morecroft. He has a thing for Holly." she said proudly to Meredith.

"Aren't you lucky?" She said enviously. She was right though. Travis was dreamy, tall and handsome with brilliant blue eyes.

"It's nice to meet you, Meredith, and we're not a thing," I clarified as I extended my hand to shake hers. "What brings you here to Appleby?"

"Mildred speaks so highly of your town, I just thought I would pop by to check it ou. I'm staying at the Lake Hotel," she said as we all continued to watch Travis through the front window.

"Meredith solved a case in Castlemeyer. Someone was breaking into houses and terrorizing the elderly. She helped catch the culprits," explained Mildred.

Through the window another police car pulled up behind Travis's vehicle and he turned the thief over to the officer. The door tinkled again as he came back inside. We turned quickly and pretended we weren't admiring his backside.

"That was a pretty good trick you pulled there Mildred but you really should be more careful or I might have to put you on the force." He winked at Mildred and she blushed.

"Aw shucks, officer, 'twasn't nuthin. Travis, I would like you to meet Meredith, she's from Castlemeyer."

"Nice to meet you," he said.

"Nice to meet you, Travis. Thanks for saving us from that awful man," she said as she playfully reached out and put her hand on his arm and my heart skipped a beat. Why couldn't I flirt with people like that? "If you're going to be in town for a while, maybe we could catch a movie or some fish?"

"Speaking of fishing. Did you hear about Pete?" asked Mildred. "Drowned in the lake, poor dear. What on earth he was doing out there at his age, I don't know. Much too cold for my poor bones." She gave a little shiver as she said it. Meredith had her lips pressed together at this little interruption. She opened her mouth to speak again when Louella jumped in.

"Detective Smart, do you know when the lake will be reopened? It's such a shame not to have the fall festival there. Did you hear that Holly is our new chairperson this year?"

All eyes turned to me, making me feel uncomfortable in the spotlight.

"I didn't know that. Congratulations Holly. Let me know what I can do to help out. I'm stationed here temporarily since Appleby is short staffed right now."

"Thank you Travis, I will let you know. Have you ever run a booth?" I asked hopefully. Now look who was flirting? Is this flirting? Maybe I should put my hand on his arm too. Meredith looked a little puzzled.

She suddenly raised her hand in the air. "I'll help," she said. "I mean it sounds like it will be fun. I wouldn't want to miss out."

"Well, thanks Meredith. I'm sure Holly can use all the help she can get. Especially since it's going to be in the haunted house." Travis winked at me as he said it.

"Haunted house?" she gulped. I totally sympathized with her, ghosts are 0not my thing. Plastering a fake smile on her face she muttered, "definitely going to be a lot of fun."

"Oh that is so sweet of you Meredith," said Mildred. "You can tell us all about your sleuthing. Won't that be wonderful Holly? You two can compare notes."

This time the fake smile was mine. "Sounds just dandy." What don't they get about 'I'm not a sleuth?'

"Well ladies, I should be getting back to the office, you know crime waits for no one." said Travis. "Louella, next time someone wants you to sign something, let Holly check it first please." Louella looked properly chastised. "Yes, sir. I will. Now don't be a stranger."

Travis gave her a peck on the cheek and walked to the door. He stopped and turned back to us. "And ladies, please stop by the station so we can get your statements. I'm sure you weren't the first ones he tried to swindle. Oh, Holly?"

"Yes, Travis?" I said, was my heart beating fast?

"Watch out for ghosts." He smiled and left out the door, the bell tinkling behind him.

Meredith turned to me. She really was a beautiful woman. "Holly, I'm sorry if I misunderstood. I thought you said the two of you weren't involved?"

"No. You're fine, we're not. Although the people in town think otherwise. Are you going to be in town long?"

Meredith lifted her long elegant arms in a shrug. "Just playing it by ear. I needed a break. Maybe we can get lunch sometime?"

"Sounds great. Tipsy's and Katie May's are both great local restaurants. I should probably be getting back to work too. If you ever need a real estate agent, I'm your gal." As I left, Mildred's voice followed me out the door.

"Louella, where are your glasses? What were you thinking trying to sign a paper you can't even read?"

Walking back to the office, my eyes drifted over to the yellow police tape off in the distance next to the lake. Poor Pete. What a way to go. Wait one doggone minute. How do you drown while ice fishing? I chewed on my bottom lip without thinking.

"Be careful or your face will get stuck that way." As I jumped, Lucy, our local title rep laughed at me. "Something exciting out here? Oh. Who's the new girl?" My eyes followed hers to the door of the candy shop where Meredith and Mildred were talking.

"She's a friend of Mildred's from Castlemeyer." Meredith looked in my direction before heading to the parking lot and waved to me. I waved back.

"Is that trollop trying to take your guy?" asked Lucy.

"What? No. He's not my guy." I frowned at her. She just raised her eyebrows in question and we both went inside.

"I hear you're chairing the Fall Festival this year and it's going to be in a haunted house." she wiggled her fingers at me and said "boo."

I sighed. "What kind of haunted are we talking about? The slasher or the ghostly kind?"

"I heard people go in and never come back out," she said in a whisper.

"Yet, we're having a festival there. Is everyone expected to disappear? That can't be true." Lucy shrugged.

I stared at her for a moment. "Hmph. Well I've got work to do. I'll talk to you later." Settling behind my desk, Lucy's question bothered me. Did I want Travis to be my guy? He was good looking, he had a job, he was in the right age bracket. The same couldn't be said for a lot of other guys around here. Typically Appleby attracted the young snow bunnies and the retirees. My friend Vana was forever trying to set me up on dates. I don't know how she landed her husband because he's a gem and these dates...were not.

I only really go on these dates to keep her at bay. One date is usually good for at least six months free of suggestions. A sudden thought made me pause. Maybe she was deliberately picking bad dates to antagonize me. Why would she do that? Putting those thoughts aside, I looked up the Blume House on the Internet and found zilch about it. How could it be haunted if there wasn't even one story about it, no murders, missing people, nothing. Maybe they were all just making it up to mess with me but why would they do that?

No matter, tonight I was going to a karate class with Mildred. If there's ghosts, I'll just kick their ghostly bottoms.

BLUME HOUSE

I spent all night tossing and turning as thoughts of ghosts kept me awake. It was probably just the stress planning for the festival plus my usual work. I'm sure it had nothing to do with a new woman interested in a man that I am not interested in. Plus all the feelings from finding out that my husband's killer was a woman I'd known for five years. How do you assuage guilt? Not a friend, but still, I had done business with her. Was she laughing behind my back the whole time? How do you not get jail time for killing two people?

At 5 am I gave up and took Ginger for a quick walk in the early morning darkness. Back home we shared some eggs and bacon. Ginger definitely enjoying it more than I. Two cups of coffee and I began to wake up. I dressed in warm clothes for my trip to the haunted house. Most likely the heat wasn't on and it was probably pretty dirty inside, having been vacant for several years.

The cloudy sky blacked the sun's warm rays this morning. As I pulled up to the Blume House, a group of ladies, dressed in thick coats and gloves, were already there waiting for me. I wasn't looking forward to going inside, not after the stories I'd heard about the place. It didn't help that the house was isolated by itself and surrounded by tall pine trees. The closest neighbor was a quarter mile away. It looked even more dark and forbidding under the overcast sky.

I groaned as I got out of the car. My first karate class with Mildred left me feeling as if every bone in my body ached. I groaned again as I saw Meredith, dressed to the nines, and Gloria approaching. Ugh, why couldn't she just join the day of the event like most of the other volunteers?

Gloria was bouncing with excitement. "This is Meredith. She's a sleuth too," she said to me.

"I'm not a sleuth," I protested. "And we've met."

"She solved my Lionel's murder," she said proudly and put her arm around my shoulder for a side hug. "It was terrifying but Detective Smart was so kind."

"Detective Smart?" Meredith asked.

"Yes! Do you know him?" Ingrid said excitedly.

Meredith nodded her head, "We've met."

"Oh, he's so handsome, isn't he Holly?" and she bumped my shoulder with her own.

"Um, yeah I guess so." I said lamely.

"You guess so?" Turning back to Meredith she added. "They had a thing going. Whatever happened to him?" she asked me.

"We didn't have a thing." I protested. "We're just acquaintances thrown together through unusual circumstances."

"I'd date him in a second," popped up Meredith.

"I'm sure you would," I muttered.

"What was that?" asked Meredith.

Oops, did I say that out loud? "I was just saying we should hurry before the ladies get lost in the woods." I locked my car and called to the women who were scattered about in little clumps. "Hello ladies. Is everyone here?"

The ladies all turned around and met me at the front of the house. The grass on the lawn was overgrown and pinecones were scattered all about. The front door was in need of paint, as were the eaves, and pretty much the entire rest of the place as well. I craned my neck looking up to the second story hoping there wasn't any movement behind any of the windows.

"Pretty spooky isn't it," said Cindy with glee. Oh it was something alright. "The mayor said they would get the lawn trimmed and spruce up the front of the house, if that's something you want."

"We thought you might like to take a look first before we had any of the spookiness taken away," piped in Patty.

Maybe it was the cold wind but I gave a little shiver. "That was so thoughtful of you but I thought this was a family friendly event."

"Oh, it is. But with Pete gone, this is a great opportunity to spook it up a little. He was against all of that and we do have to replace the ice skating now." Cindy finished up her little spiel with a sad pouty face.

I do not do spooky. "Why don't we take a look inside first and see what ideas come to mind," I suggested.

"Oh, we can't go in yet," called out another woman as she pushed her way to the front.

"We can't?" I asked.

"No. Louella has the keys. She called me this morning and said she would be here bright and early but I haven't seen her yet."

"I don't see her car," said another.

"You wouldn't, she said she was getting a ride," answered the first woman who turned out to be Carol Whiteside, the blonde woman who handed out the papers at the planning meeting.

"Carol right?"

"Yes, I'm so happy you're taking over. Pete could be a curmudgeon sometimes. You see, we wanted to use this house before but nooo, not Pete. Anyway, maybe we should take a look. Louella likes to go walking."

My foot kicked something in the weeds and I bent down to investigate. It was an old pair of eyeglasses and I picked them up. They were horribly scratched and must have been here for quite a while.

"Those are Louella's," exclaimed Patty. "She must have dropped them."

My eyebrows rose in surprise. How could she see through them? Maybe someone had stepped on them after she dropped them. I almost did. "Yes, why don't we all grab a partner or two and see if we can find her. Without her glasses, maybe she got lost."

"I'll go check out along the cliff," piped up Meredith.

"Oh, she would never go that way without her glasses." Carol shook her head as she spoke. "She can't see two feet in front of her without them." I looked at the glasses in my hand. The lenses were quite thick. My brain was telling me there was something I should remember but the full thought wouldn't come.

Meredith shrugged and flicked her hair back over her shoulder. "It doesn't hurt to be thorough and I've heard the view is fantastic." She headed off to the cliffs with Gloria and the rest of us scattered into groups of two and three to search for Louella.

How hard could it be to find an old woman in her eighties? I checked the front door but it was still locked as were all the other doors into the house. Several of the ladies walked back along the road and the others took a path off to the side of the house. After checking all the doors, I followed along the dirt path which led through the woods for a short distance before the trees opened up into a stunning view of the valley. A sudden scream hurried me along the path.

Gloria, Meredith and Carol were gathered at the edge of the cliff and peering over the side. "It's poor Louella," cried Meredith. "I can just see her arm sticking out from the brush."

"We called out to her, but she didn't answer. Do you think she's okay?" worried Gloria.

Stepping carefully to the edge and using Gloria's arm for leverage, I peered over as well and could see where brush had been torn out as something fell through it. About half way down the hill, a small arm was visible. There was no way I would have survived the fall, let alone an elderly woman. The ground was damp and spongy and my heart dropped as my foot slipped in the mud. Time seemed to stand still as half of me was suspended over the drop before Meredith pulled us back from the edge.

"Be careful Holly. We don't want you down there," she admonished me.

I pulled my phone from my purse and called 911. "It's much too steep. We'll just have to wait for emergency personnel to get here," I said looking at the women. Carol had her hands over her mouth and Meredith had her arm around Gloria to comfort her. It wouldn't do to have everyone find out this way. "Ladies, please go back to the cars and let everyone know to stay there until the police get here. They're going to need to have room to work. I'll wait here for them."

"Quite right," said Carol as she grabbed Meredith and Gloria's arms. "Let's get back before anyone else gets here."

The silence was overwhelming after the women left. An icy wind came up the hillside and I wrapped my jacket tighter around me. The view was beautiful but the area seemed desolate in the aftermath of the tragedy. Blume House definitely had a ghost now.

As soon as the emergency personnel arrived, I rejoined the rest of the ladies at the house where an officer was taking their statements. One voice rose above the others.

"Oh officers, it's simply dreadful," wailed Meredith with tears in her eyes. "Such a nice old lady."

Gloria was standing near the edge of the group rubbing her side when I joined her. "Are you okay?"

"Ah, don't mind me, it's just my hip. Whenever the weather gets cold it aches," she answered. "A nice warm tub and I'll be as good as gold."

I nodded towards Meredith. "She seems a bit shaken up. I didn't think she knew Louella."

"She doesn't, she only met her at the candy shop. She's just a tad dramatic if you know what I mean."

A hand on my shoulder made me shriek. "I'm sorry, I didn't mean to scare you," said Travis. "Can we talk away from the group?" He inclined his head toward the parking area.

"Sure."

His face was grim as we walked a few paces away from the others. "I'm sure you've guessed she didn't survive. They're still recovering the body. It might take awhile. Do you know why she was out there alone?"

"No. Carol said she arrived early, maybe she got bored waiting?"

"What time were you all supposed to arrive?"

"Eleven o'clock. I guess this means we'll have to find a new location for the festival now."

Travis gave me a strange look. "Why would you need to do that?"

I looked back at him equally puzzled. "Because someone died? The festival was originally moved because Pete died at the lake."

"Oh." His face looked quite grim.

"Oh, what?"

He looked at me a moment before speaking as if trying to find the right words. "Pete was partially frozen into the lake. They've had a hard time removing his body."

"Oh." I guess that would make things difficult.

"There was that sudden freeze and I guess he just wasn't prepared for it."

"What do you mean?" I asked before getting interrupted by the officer who had been taking the statements.

"I've told the women to all go home." He was one of the younger officers in town. "One of them, Meredith, said she's too shaken up to drive and asked if she could get a ride home. I'm heading back now," he said hopefully.

"Sure. Can you give her a ride? I'm going to be tied up here for a while," responded Travis.

"Sure thing boss," said the officer waggling his eyebrows as he walked off.

Travis hid a laugh. "Such a flirt. Did Meredith know Louella?"

I just raised my eyebrows and shrugged. "I just met the woman. You said Pete was frozen into the lake? But the ladies said he was going ice fishing, wouldn't that mean the lake had to be frozen first?"

He held my gaze with his brilliant blue eyes. "Holly."

Suddenly I didn't want to know what he had to say. "I know, it's not my place to ask questions. You know I've got to be going anyway. I'll see you around." Turning, I walked back to my car. Getting in, I fastened my seatbelt and drove away without bothering to look back. And then I kicked myself mentally. What was I so afraid of?

A BREAK IN

Appleby is a quaint mountain town where everyone knows each other and helps each other out, with the exception of the tourists. Most of them were alright, courteous for the most part, but there were the few that caused problems. Most times they didn't come back for a second visit. As I said, we watch out for each other.

As a real estate agent, I suppose I feel more of an obligation to keep my small community safe. It's not just for business either, I raised my daughter here and now my granddaughter, Chloe, lives here too. She and her friends deserve a safe place to call home.

My house sits up on a hill, in a small neighborhood, where the houses aren't too close together, but close enough to visit within walking distance. I like to take a walk in the afternoon, when the weather is nice, like today. I snuck out without Ginger, because frankly, she's huge and chases the squirrels away. It was quite the stressful day today and I needed some me time.

I headed down the street toward Mildred's house for some flower therapy. The front garden was just a riot of colors and smells. There were flowers I'd never seen before. This late in the year, they should all be gone but Mildred has a surprisingly green thumb.

I first met Mildred at the candy shop in town years ago and she has always been an exceptional proprietor but now I'm actually a little jealous of her gardening abilities. It's been ten years and I still haven't planted roses in front of my home. A beautiful orange rose that looked like it glowed in the sunlight caught my eye and I leaned over the short, white picket fence and inhaled deeply. I was rewarded with disappointment. No fragrance. So many nowadays don't have good fragrances, instead they are bred for their beauty. Oh well, the deep burgundy ones always smelled good but I would have to go inside her gate, which was open, to smell them.

I suppose it seems a bit ridiculous to invade someone's property just to smell flowers but if you can't stop and smell the roses periodically, what's the point of life? Besides, I could check in on her and maybe have a bit of conversation over tea. Perhaps she had an update on Pete and Louella, after all, the candy store was basically, the office water cooler. Everybody talked about everything there.

I closed my eyes and inhaled deeply. The scent of the Mirandy rose was everything I was expecting, a deep fragrant, rose scent. As I raised my head and opened my eyes, a glint of sunlight on water caught my eye. Well that's weird. The hose was lying on the grass, water running freely from the nozzle.

Mildred was very water conscious, she would never leave the hose running. Worried something might be wrong, I hurried around to the front door. It looked closed but as I pressed my hand against it to knock, it swung open. I meant to call out her name, and I can't tell you why, but in that moment, I didn't. Instead I stepped quietly into the living room. Knick knacks lined shelves and curio cabinets in the small comfortable room. The kitchen was visible through one door, and a hall led back to the bedrooms and bath. It was small but comfortable.

Really, this is silly, what if I caught her coming out of the bath. Maybe she had to run to answer the phone, as she still only had a landline. Mildred was old enough to still relish the silence that came with not carrying a mobile phone around. Still, she would have taken the time to shut off the water, the faucet was right next to the front door. Mentally, kicking myself for not shutting the water off myself, I froze as a loud angry voice rang out from the back bedroom.

"Where's the money, old woman?" My anger rose. First of all, no one talked to Mildred like that and secondly, no one was intruding on my neighbor's house to rob the place. Wishing I had brought Ginger with me, I took a second to grab a weapon from the kitchen. Cell reception was spotty here as Mildred also had no wifi and a quick glance showed I had no signal. Although she didn't like mobile phones, she did have a phone that wasn't connected to the wall and was unfortunately, nowhere in sight.

A short shriek from Mildred let me know that time was quickly running out. Tiptoeing down the hall, I leaned back against the wall and took a quick peek through the bedroom door. The door was partially shut but through the crack I could see poor Mildred cowering on the floor with her hands held up near her face. The intruder's back was to me and I could see he wore a ski mask over his head. Outrage flooded through me. That man better not have hurt her! Filled with righteous indignation, I stepped up behind the man and swung the weapon in my hands with all my strength.

Focussed as he was on his victim, he didn't hear me and that was his downfall. The extra large cast iron pan I held cracked him against the back of his head and he crumpled to the ground unconscious as Mildred rolled away.

"How do you move like that," I marveled as I helped Mildred to her feet. I had taken a karate class with her but I couldn't move like that and I was nearly 30 years younger.

"I may be old but I'm not helpless," she said as she gave me a hug. "Thank you for coming to my rescue. Now I'm sure I have some old clothesline around here to tie this guy up."

"I should call the police," I said to her."Where's your phone?"

"Don't bother, they should be here any minute." Opening my mouth to speak, she answered my unasked question by holding up her arm. A glittery bracelet adorned her wrist. "It's my alert bracelet. I just press the button and they send someone out if I don't answer the phone."

A smile creased my lips, "you are always full of surprises." A furious scratching at the door made us both jump. "Is that a bear?" I whispered loudly. Mildred poked her head through the curtain at the front window and then opened the front door and stood out of the way as a large dark shape barreled through and ran into the bedroom. When it didn't return, Mildred and I looked at each other and then followed it into the bedroom where we found Ginger lying across the thief and whining.

"Ginger! What are you doing here?" I asked in surprise and then looked at her sternly as I remembered Ben telling me about her jumping the fence.

"Don't be too rough on her," said Mildred scratching the dog's ears. "She came to your rescue you know."

The wonderment of it struck me a moment later. "How do you think she knew?"

Mildred shook her head. "Animals are strange creatures. They know things we don't." Ginger just looked up at me accusingly with her big brown eyes, making me feel guilty for not bringing her.

A few moments later and a paramedic was poking his head around the door. "Miss Beaumont, do you require assistance?"

"No young man, but the intruder here is gonna need some help. I'm pretty sure Holly here gave him a concussion." With a puzzled look on his face, he leaned into the radio on his chest and called for police assistance as his partner followed him into the bedroom. The police showed up ten minutes later and handcuffed the still unconscious intruder to the ambulance gurney.

"My grandma always told me how useful cast iron pans were. Never thought I'd see one used like this though," said police Detective David Martin as he spun the pan in his hand like a basketball before handing it to Mildred and winking at her. "You better take this. Just in case anyone else comes around."

"Don't you usually investigate crimes?" Mildred asked with a little frown.

"I was in the neighborhood, there's been a rash of break-ins lately. This guy probably belongs to the same gang. I'm just glad you're alright."

Now it was my turn to frown, "how come we haven't heard about this?"

"They've been empty cabins until now and we're pretty sure that's all it was until now."

Mildred huffed. "Well I hope you're going to send out an alert now."

Detective Martin looked apologetic. "If we thought this might happen, we would have done it sooner. My apologies. Do you know what he wanted?"

My Scoobydar perked up at the question. "He was looking for money," I said before Mildred could answer. "What else would it be?"

"Sometimes, they're looking for drugs. What exactly did he say?" He looked directly at Mildred as he asked.

"Where's your money old woman," she said in a wobbly voice which made me look curiously at her. "If you don't mind, I'd like to lie down for a bit, this has been very traumatic." She put her hand to her chest and appeared every bit her age.

"Of course," he handed me his card. "If you remember anything else that can help or if you hear anything around your house, just give me a call." He closed the front door behind him as he left and shortly after, the vehicles drove away.

I turned to Mildred with my eyebrows raised, "I'm pretty sure his exact words were, 'where's the money'."

Mildred just went, "hmph. I guess I just got the words twisted around. I'm going to lie down, I really am tired and please lock the door when you leave. Oh, and turn off the water, like a good dear."

"Sure thing Mildred. I'll be back to check on you later." Perhaps it was nothing or maybe it was something. What I did know was that I would have to wait till later to find out. I grabbed Ginger and the two of us made our way home. After turning off the water, of course.

HAUNTED HOUSE

It was three days later and Mildred had suffered no ill effects from the intrusion. Ben had come over and helped to install a roller bar along the top edge of my fence to stop Ginger from jumping over. Part of me was conflicted about it though as she had come to my rescue by jumping over the fence. I gave her some extra treats to ease my pain.

Today, I was meeting the committee ladies at the Blume house to go inside and decide how we wanted to set up for the fall festival. Part of me was disappointed that Louella's death hadn't canceled the event. Maybe it wouldn't be as scary on the inside as it looked like on the outside.

Maybe I should bring Ginger with me. She would chase any ghosts away. I looked down at her big brown eyes as she cocked her head sideways at me. Naw, that wouldn't be fair to the dog. "It's okay," I said petting her. "I'm a big girl, I can handle this. And it's not like I'm going to be alone right? I mean what could happen with a bunch of women in an old house?"

As I drove away, I could see her watching me out the window. Thankfully, today was bright and sunny, not a cloud in the sky. I tried to focus on the beautiful scenery as I drove up the winding mountain road to the Blume house.

Carol, Gloria, Mildred, Meredith, Cindy, Tabitha and I all gathered together on the front porch of the Blume House, so named for the original settlers who built it. Not much was known about them, except that they had a lot of money at the time.

"Good morning ladies, so nice to see you all bright and early this morning," I greeted them. Although it was sunny and early, it wasn't too bright here on the porch where the house was overshadowed by huge pine trees. I was definitely not looking forward to entering a house that was rumored to be haunted.

The sound of tires crunching on gravel interrupted our entrance as we all looked to see who was arriving. Like a clown emerging at a circus, a very tall woman dressed in a plaid shirt and jeans emerged from the tiny little smart car.

"Oh, no," sighed Mildred behind me. "That's Maggie Moore. Maggs for short. She's quite a handful."

"You mean a complainer," piped up Carol. I felt a hand pat me on the shoulder and I glanced behind to see Gloria.

"It's okay," she whispered, "you can handle her. You're a real estate agent."

"What's that supposed to mean?" I whispered back at her with a smile on my face for the woman approaching.

"You're used to handling difficult people. It's like part of your job description. Hello, Maggs." She ended her comment in a loud voice as Maggs reached the steps.

"Well, I guess the ladies already introduced me, without me being present." She spoke in a matter of fact voice as if this happened all the time. I extended my hand to her.

"Hi. I'm Holly Holcraft and I'm the chairperson this year."

Ignoring my hand, she nodded her head instead. "I know who you are. I just hope you do half as good a job as Pete did. Poor Pete." She shook her head sadly. "He was a great guy, a real advocate for the disabled ever since he broke both his legs. Did you know he had to have rods put in both legs?" She looked at me expectantly.

'Uh, no, I didn't know that," I replied.

"I didn't think so. So, we gonna get this shindig going or what?"

Well, okay then. I could see how this was gonna go. I have found that two techniques work with complainers, either ignore the complaints or have a firm hand with the complainer. I figure I'll try ignoring the complaints for now and see how that goes. "Thanks for joining us Maggie. I'm just opening the door now. I look forward to hearing about your ideas for the festival this year," I said, as I inserted the key the mayor's secretary had gotten me, in the front door and pushed it open. We never did find Louella's key. It must still be out in the brush somewhere. Someone will find it someday, all old and rusty, and never know the tragedy behind it. The porch boards groaned under my feet. "After you," I added and stepped to the side to allow the ladies through.

Unlike me, they seemed eager to enter the forbidding house, just another clue that there weren't really any ghosts. I followed them and was shocked to discover not a speck of dust inside. I guess the surprise showed on my face because Cindy piped up. "The Mayor had a full crew in here to clean up for us."

I frowned. "Why do you look disappointed? Did you want to clean it?"

"Oh no, said Gloria. "But what's a haunted house without dust?"

"Um, clean?" I responded. "Maybe the ghosts don't like dirt. Besides, it's still dark and spooky in here." I gestured around the space. Directly in front of the door was a massive staircase running to the second floor. Hallways opened up to wings on either side of the main room, paneled in dark wood and with heavy drapes over the windows, resulting in a very dismal place. "Let's take a look around and you ladies can pick out the areas you want to set up in."

That set off an instant uproar as the ladies all began making dibs on the areas they wanted. Carol and Meredith set off for the second floor, Tabitha headed for the atrium and Cindy, Gloria, Mildred, Maggs and I set out to explore the ground floor. We headed for the kitchen and dining room first so we would know what we were going to have to work with.

Most of the rooms were empty, but a few still had a few Victorian pieces. The dining room featured a huge buffet against the wall and a fireplace but no tables or chairs, while the kitchen was absolutely outstanding. Someone had lived here not too long ago because it had a functioning stove and a large island. Large windows looked out upon the backyard and what I guessed was the atrium off to the left. A fairly large lawn was inundated with weeds but that could be cleared out and would make a lovely place for games, providing the weather cooperated.

"You know," said Maggs, with her arms crossed and her chin resting on her hand. "We could probably make an ice skating rink out there."

"Why that's a wonderful idea," exclaimed Mildred. "Some of the kids in the candy shop were so disappointed about the ice skating. I think you should be in charge of that. Don't you think so Holly?"

I jumped in before Maggs had a chance to back out. "Why that is a wonderful idea. Thank you for handling that for us Maggie." Maggie looked back and forth between us with her mouth open.

"Okay," she finally said. "And call me Maggs."

Bear!" whispered Cindy loudly . I peered through the window at the backyard, not seeing anything.

"I don't see anything?"

"Not out there," she cried pointing behind us. "There!"

A large bear was silhouetted in the doorway to the kitchen so the five of us very, very slowly edged towards the back door, which was locked, with a keyed deadbolt. I slid the keys into Maggs' hand and she reached behind her and tried to fit it into the lock. The bear meanwhile was shuffling around the island towards the stove making snuffily noises. "Hurry up," I encouraged in a loud whisper.

"I'm working as fast as I can," Maggs whispered back frantically trying each key. "The keys don't fit." The bear reared up on its hind legs to check out the top of the counter and then turned its head and looked at us. There was a collective gasp as we all froze.

"There!" cried Gloria pointing. "That door." We all looked at the door she indicated as the bear growled. Without a second thought, we all sprinted for the door. Maggs reached it first and threw it open as the rest of us barreled through and then down the stairs that were there. Gloria slammed it shut behind us.

We all cowered in what I imagined was the cellar. The bear scratched and banged at the door making it bounce in the frame. Dirt rained down from the ceiling.

I looked around the space desperately for an exit. It was lined floor to ceiling with shelves and junk. Unfortunately, there were no windows. We had to be below ground level. Suddenly Cindy chortled.

"Is that a door?" She pointed to a section of shelving. It definitely didn't look like a door. Cindy ran her fingers around the frame and the shelves slid out from the wall. "Quick everybody in."

"Oh, I don't think we should go in there," began Mildred but we were already diving through the opening into the blackness beyond. The very solid blackness.

"Don't shut the door all the way," I yelled just as we all heard a definite click as Cindy pulled it shut. I pushed past the ladies and tried to open it but the door was closed, shut tight. Locked. As hard as I pushed and banged, there was no getting through it. "Why would you shut that?" I directed at Cindy.

"The bear?" She said with a shrug.

"Ladies, turn on the lights on your cell phones." The sudden brilliance made us blink. The illumination revealed rough hewn walls. "Are we in a cave?" I asked.

"I can't hear the bear anymore," whispered Cindy.

"There's another opening this way," called Gloria from a few feet away.

"Then I guess we have no other choice but to find what's at the other end," commented Maggs.

"Oh no," said Mildred. "We should probably just stay here. Carol, Tabitha and Meredith will come looking for us."

I looked down at my phone. No signal. "Do any of you ladies have a signal?"

"No," was repeated down the line.

"Well, what do you ladies want to do?" I asked.

"I vote we search for a way out," put in Maggs.

"I second that," said Cindy. "I don't like dark places."

"It'll be an adventure," piped up Gloria. She was always a bit too upbeat sometimes. Mildred just sighed.

"Okay, then. Let's check out the tunnel. Maggs, you want to do the honors?" I asked.

"Why do I have to go first?"

"Because you have the best eyesight," remarked Cindy. Maggs looked around at the ladies and landed on me.

"You're taller and can see farther," I said before she had a chance to talk. She shrugged and accepted her fate.

"Maybe we don't all want to use our lights at the same time. We don't know how long this tunnel is," she commented before turning and walking on.

Three of the lights flashed out, including mine. Maggs kept hers on at the front of the group and Cindy had hers on at the back. Now the dark seemed to close in on all sides and I realized I now knew what they meant by the sound of silence. It was pretty scary. The haunted house had nothing on this place. A part of me wished I'd stomped on the part of me that didn't want to bring Ginger with me this morning.

Gloria's voice cut the silence. "Hey, maybe we should include this as part of the festival." I was beginning to think she was a scare junkie. We continued to walk on in silence, the air getting chillier the farther we ventured.

"Ladies," came Magg's voice. "It looks like there was a cave-in in here recently, the rocks are scattered across the floor. Watch your step."

"Oh, It's a good thing Tabitha didn't get caught down here with us," said Gloria. "She hurt her foot wearing the wrong shoes the other day and she's been hobbling around since then."

"Wearing the wrong shoes? That's a thing?" I asked.

"Oh that's nothing, sprained my hip one day leaning over to pick up a book off the shelf," added Mildred. "Getting old sucks."

"This cold isn't helping either," complained Maggs. "At my age, I don't care how I look, comfort is everything. Do any of you have an extra jacket? I didn't know we were going to be cave hiking and I didn't bring one." As if anyone could really have predicted this.

"Oh you should get a jacket like mine, it's so warm but still stylish," said Cindy, stopping to twirl in the tunnel. She posed a few times and reached up to pat the bottom of her hair. Maggs came back when she saw we weren't following her. I saw the 30 degrees logo on her jacket.

"But your jacket says 30 degrees on it. Doesn't that mean it's good for that temperature?"

"Well it's not," cut in Gloria. "It really needs a layer of wool for insulation. That's just the company name."

"Oh, I didn't realize that," I said. Cindy stopped preening and we continued on in silence.

"Gloria, you know, I was wondering something," I said after a few moments.

"Yes?"

"I thought you lived in Morecroft," I said puzzled. After all, that was where her boyfriend had lived.

Gloria shrugged. "I needed a change of pace and the ladies here are just amazing."

"Oh. Where did you meet Meredith?"

"Years ago. It was a book club in Castlemeyer. I don't think they even meet anymore. The building was condemned."

"Is anyone else from Castlemeyer?"

"Oh, just Carol. She moved here after her husband died. Although she was never in the book club. Speaking of books, have you read the latest Ophelia Love book?"

"Um, isn't that spicy romance?"

"It is but it's so delicious. It just came out last night."

"Last night? And you already have it?"

"Oh, yes. I read it on my Kindle." She continued on at my blank look. "You know electronically. It just got released at midnight and I stayed up nearly the whole night reading it." She signed dramatically. "If only I could be the plot of a spicy romance. I can't wait for the next one." She then sashayed down the tunnel with her arms wrapped around her.

Won't she be disappointed when that next book doesn't come out. I watched her until I realized the darkness was surrounding me and then hurried after her. A tunnel is no place to be lost in the dark. We continued on. The ground gradually began sloping upward. At one point Maggs' light disappeared ahead. "Maggs, you okay up there?" I called out concerned.

"Sure thing," came back the reply. "Although, I could use some water. Don't suppose you ladies thought to grab some?"

"Are we going in circles?" I asked the ladies.

"Only Magg's questions," came back down the tunnel. It was so hard to tell direction in the dark. A dark opening loomed to the right of our tunnel. Definitely not going in a circle then. I shivered and pulled my suit jacket tighter around my body. The dampness and cold had a way of soaking into my skin. Or maybe the darkness was making it seem colder than it really was. It felt like we'd been walking for hours.

"Do we keep going left or should we try to the right?" asked Maggs.

"Definitely stay on the left," said Mildred in a resigned voice. What was wrong with her anyway? "If we keep changing direction, we could get lost in here."

She had a point there. The ladies all looked to me for an answer. "Um, that sounds good. If there's nothing up ahead, we can always come back." In the silence that followed my statement, I heard a scratching noise. The hair on my neck rose and a chill ran over me. I looked around but saw nothing. "Did you hear that?" I asked.

"Hear what?" said several voices.

"I thought I heard a noise behind us," I said.

"What?" asked Maggs.

"She said she thinks she heard something," explained Cindy in a louder voice. "Is your hearing going?"

"Oh, you don't think it's the bear do you?" Gloria asked, sounding strangely hopeful.

"It had better not be," exclaimed Maggs. "I've had about as much as I can stand already. And my hearing is just fine, thank you."

"Shush," I said loudly. "Let's just listen for a second." The ladies clamped their mouths closed and we listened, but there wasn't so much as a breeze blowing through. "I guess I was mistaken. Let's get going again."

"Thanks for the moment of silence," snarked Maggs. I was beginning to see what the ladies had meant about Maggs. We continued on into the darkness, a little more apprehensive than before. The dark opening lingering in my mind. What if there was a bear in here with us?

As we rounded what had to be a curve, we found Maggs sitting down with her back against the wall. "You girls go ahead, I'm done." I looked at her in disbelief.

"Okay, fine," I responded shortly. "Maggs is done. Let's go." Shocked faces looked back at me. "Seriously, she said she's done and I respect people's opinions, so we'll just leave her here. She'll be fine as long as the battery on her phone lasts. I'm sure the anticipation of a catastrophe is infinitely worse than the real thing so let's go." The ladies all nodded numbly and walked past her down the tunnel, Gloria flicking on her light and taking the lead. The darkness crept closer to Maggs.

"Wait. Wait!" Maggs rolled on to her knees, then put a hand against the clammy cave wall and slowly rose to her feet. "Maybe I was a bit hasty. I think I'll try for just a bit longer."

I waited for Maggs to catch up. When she did, she slapped my shoulder with her hand.

"What the heck was that? You're supposed to give me a rousing speech of encouragement. Not just leave me behind."

"The end result was the same and we don't have time to waste on your shenanigans. Trapped in a damp tunnel that has collapsed in the past is clearly NOT the place and if you feel that I'm wrong, then you clearly need to reevaluate your priorities." I think the silent tunnel was beginning to wear on my civilities.

Anger and shame battled for prominence on her face before acceptance finally won. "And," I continued. "Perhaps you need to learn the difference between positive and negative attention. If you do anything like this again, I will leave you behind without hesitation. I, for one, have reasons to live and I won't let you jeopardize that because of your need for attention. Are we clear?"

After several attempts to speak, Maggs finally settled on just one word, "yes," then humbly followed the ladies up the tunnel.

"Shhh," whispered Gloria. "Do you hear that?"

"Yeah, we already did that," said Maggs.

"Shhh," exclaimed Gloria looking back down the tunnel. "There's something in the dark." Then we all heard it, a scratching noise and then a hiss. That's when we all turned and ran pell mell until we all crashed into each other. We had reached the end.

The tunnel ended strangely enough, at a wooden door. "Well would you look at that?" exclaimed Maggs in wonder. "What is a door doing here?"

"I should think you would be happy enough to find an exit," muttered Cindy as she searched for the handle. "Found the handle." All hands suddenly grabbed for it.

"Ladies! Let's keep calm and see if we can even open the door," I said as the voice of reason. Reaching out, I grasped the ice cold handle and gave a turn. Nothing, nada. The door handle was locked tight. "It's locked."

"We could all grab Maggs and use her as a battering ram. Her hard head should break through in no time," remarked Cindy.

"Great suggestion Cindy but let's look around and see if there's anything we can use to pry the door open first," I suggested to keep them busy. All the lights suddenly flashed on and the ladies immediately began to look around, giving frantic looks down the dark tunnel.

Maggs screamed. "Something brushed my leg," she squealed. All the lights immediately pointed at the ground.

"Why, it's just a cat. Come here little kitty," cooed Cindy at the solid black creature. While they all ooo'd and awed over the cat I gave the lock a closer examination. It was one of those old fashioned locks that used an old key that was round on top and rectangular on the bottom. It looked familiar. What would the chances be? Naw, couldn't be. Even if it did fit, it would probably break when I turned it. I pulled on the chain around my neck and lifted the old brass key with the gold floral flourishes and slipped it into the lock. Hesitating for a moment, I closed my eyes in a prayer and turned the key. The door opened with a quiet click.

"I think I've got it," I said, probably a bit too loudly because the ladies all jumped. I watched the lights bouncing around the walls.

"Well open the door," they all yelled at once.

I put out my fingertips and pushed against the door which swung inwards silently. "Well that's weird."

"What is?" asked Mildred.

"It's like the hinges have been oiled. Someone has been using this cave as an entrance."

"Or an exit." stated Cindy. I looked at her with wide eyes, something niggling at the back of my brain.

"Let's go!" yelled a voice behind me and someone shoved me forward through the door. They fell all over themselves to get inside and then slammed it shut behind them.

The door emptied out into a cellar just like the one we had left, what seemed ages ago. I turned around and looked at the door after all the ladies came through. It had shelves on the other side to hide it as well. Across the room, a wooden staircase led to another closed door.

"Oh, oh," someone cried.

"What now?" I asked.

"The cat ran off."

"Probably for the best." I said, taking a chance to look around.

"Cindy, how did you know that was a door?" I asked. When shut, it blended in perfectly with the wall.

Cindy shrugged. "I just love old houses and their secret passages. I once took a tour through a castle that had lots of them like this."

"You don't suppose that bear came up here too," interrupted Mildred. "Maybe we shouldn't go in." We all looked at her puzzled.

Gloria went over to her and put her arm around her shoulder. "We don't even know where here is. I'm sure we'll be just fine."

Mildred pushed her way over to me. "Maybe Holly and I should go up first, just to be sure." She looked around the group and waited for the ladies to nod their heads back at her. "Great. We'll come back down and let you ladies know it's safe."

I just looked at her bewildered. She did know karate though so I guessed she could handle anything but this was going to make two houses in a row that I didn't want to enter. If this was even a house. Anything could be behind that door. On second thought, maybe

Maggs should go with Mildred. As I contemplated this idea, Mildred grabbed my arm and drug me up the stairs.

The door was unlocked and Mildred thrust me through it and then shut it firmly behind her.

"Are you okay?" I looked at her puzzled. "You've been acting a little strange since we got locked in the cellar."

A chair scraped the floor behind me and Mildred's eyes shifted to look over my shoulder. I turned as well and stopped in shock. The sight before me had me absolutely floored.

A REVELATION

"**B**etty? You're supposed to be dead," I said in total shock. She gave me a sheepish grin. We were in another kitchen. Brilliant sunlight came through the lace curtains and the aroma of baking cookies assailed my nostrils adding to the surreal air.

"What are you doing here?" She asked holding a cup of tea halfway to her mouth.

"A bear came into the house while we were setting up for the fall festival," explained Mildred calmly as if it was an everyday occurrence.

"At the Blume house? What happened to the lake?"

"Pete was found in the lake," jumped in Mildred again. Betty's eyebrows rose. My eyes ping ponged back and forth between the two of them, too shocked still to speak. "He'd been in for some time, the fish had been nibbling at him. How ironic, him fishing and the fish ate him." She looked suddenly contrite. "Sorry."

"What was Pete doing fishing? He hates fish," declared Betty. "How do you know he was fishing?"

"Well, Meredith said..." began Mildred but Betty cut in, "Meredith Maroney?"

"Yes, well she saw the pole and the chair."

I finally found my voice. "How do you know her?" I asked Betty.

She waved her hand in the air as if it was of no consequence but she looked worried. "I used to know her back in the day. I suppose you got in with the key I left for you?" She stated it so matter of factly, like I was eventually going to figure it out. Next to her was a woman I'd never seen before sipping a cup of tea as well.

"How are you still alive?" Even as I said it, it made me angry. I was devastated when she died. It had happened so quickly after I met her and began to like her, that I felt cheated when I was told she was gone. "I went to your funeral."

"Come sit down. And I'll explain everything."

"Oh no, we can't," piped up Mildred. "The other ladies are downstairs in the cellar. They'll be coming up any moment. You've got to hide. Quickly." The door handle jiggled and Mildred grabbed it and held it tight.

The two ladies at the table looked at each other. The stranger patted Betty's arm. "It's okay. You go upstairs and hide in my bedroom. I'll handle this." Betty looked worried but the woman gave her a nudge and nodded assuringly.

Betty disappeared down the hall and Mildred let go of the cellar door handle. The other ladies spilled into the bright sunny kitchen. "Oh dear, the handle was stuck," she said as the ladies looked at her accusingly.

"It's about time," said Cindy brushing at her clothes. "What have you been doing up here? Social hour?" She stepped over to the stranger at the table who was feigning surprise at the appearance of the women. "Hello, I'm Cindy and these women and I were all stuck in the tunnel."

"A bear came in the house, you know," added Gloria.

Maggs slumped exhausted into a chair. "If you don't mind," she said. "My name is Maggs. We must've walked for miles."

"Um, well it's not everyday women pop into my kitchen from the cellar. Would you like a cup of tea?" she asked as she rose from the table and busied herself getting cups from the cupboard and filling the tea kettle, we settled ourselves at the table. "My name is Daria Greay. I just moved in. How did you get into my cellar?"

"Oh, there's a tunnel connecting this house to the Blume house but the door got locked behind us when the bear came in the kitchen," explained Cindy, fanning her face. "It was so exciting."

Daria turned from the stove and set the cups on the table. She was dressed in jeans and a floral button down shirt. There was a preciseness about her every movement. "There's a tunnel in my cellar? Should I be worried about this?"

Wow, she was good. My mind was filled with a thousand questions. As my eye caught Mildred's, she gave a brief shake of her head. Apparently, I was getting no answers today. My phone chimed. "I guess we've got a phone signal again. Where are we?" I directed to Daria.

"Well, if you came from the Blume house, then you're up the hill from there. My house is directly above it." She looked at Maggs before adding. "It's only a quarter mile or so from the Blume house." She directed her next question to Cindy. "There's a door in my cellar? I've never seen one."

"Oh, yes. It's just like those haunted castles," Cindy said excitedly. "We should make it part of the festival."

"Oh no, I don't think so. Tunnels are best kept secret," stated Mildred.

"Yes please, I mean no. I mean, I don't want to have to worry about people sneaking into my house," replied Daria.

And I didn't want them to know about my key. "Why don't we just keep this a secret amongst ourselves," I added.

"But what will we tell the other ladies?" Gloria questioned. Hmm, she was right. How do we explain this? To stall answering I looked at the message on my phone. It was from Meredith.

"Where are you guys?"

The ladies were all looking at me for an answer. "That was Meredith. She doesn't know where we are. Could we just walk back down the road and say we got lost?" They all turned to Daria who rubbed her neck with her hand and then squinched up her face.

"Well. It's not that far by road and it's all downhill." She looked at us doubtfully. We were pretty disheveled and tired. "If you could make it, that is. I'd really prefer to keep the tunnel secret."

Maggs looked exhausted but I was beginning to think she was just a great actor. Cindy just looked excited. Gloria and Mildred were the oldest and they looked like they were doing fine. I certainly could walk a bit more, especially if it was downhill. Was the Blume house jinxed or what?

"I'm up for it. If you ladies are." I looked around the table at each one of them in turn.

"Okay, fine," declared Maggs. "I'll have a go. But after a cup of tea. Meredith can just wait."

"I'll just text her and let her know we'll be there shortly."

"Shortly?" questioned Mildred.

"Hey, I'm a real estate agent. Time is relative." The ladies all burst out laughing, then we enjoyed fresh oatmeal cookies and hot tea. Daria was a delight. She described herself as an adventurer and she certainly looked the part, slim and in her 40's, she regaled us with tales of hiking in different countries. She had moved here to write a memoir of her adventures figuring the isolation would keep her on track.

After too many cookies and tea, we all used the restroom before starting back. As my mother always said, you should never skip an opportunity to use the restroom. It was sage advice that Lucy should have followed before we got stuck in the escape room last month.

"WHERE HAVE YOU BEEN?" Tabitha's voice assailed our ears as we rounded the corner of the house. The trip back had been pretty uneventful except for the occasional rustling noise which sent all of us into a panic each time. We'd decided to cut across the backyard as we got closer to help evade suspicion. She stood at the side of the house with her hands on her hips. "We've been looking everywhere for you. We're supposed to be getting the place ready."

Meredith popped out of the house. "I'm sorry, Tabitha. They just texted me back a few minutes ago."

Maggs raised her eyebrows at Tabitha. "Aren't you afraid the bear might come back?"

"Bear? What bear?"

"There was a bear in the kitchen. We ran out the backdoor to get away and then got lost in the woods," explained Cindy. She was right on point with what we had decided to say. The other ladies all nodded in confirmation.

"There are no bears here," said Tabitha matter of factly. "I should know."

"And how's that?" I asked. I couldn't resist calling her on her lie.

"I have traveled extensively in this area and haven't seen one yet. Look, if you guys don't want to work, fine. I can take over."

I could see that Tabitha was going to be a handful. She might look like everyone's little sister with her brown hair in a ponytail and wearing jeans and a pink flannel shirt but she definitely had an attitude. "There was a bear," I stated firmly. "Whether you believe it or not. Mildred, do you know anyone that could help out with keeping the bear away during the festival?" I turned my back on Tabitha to address her.

"Oh, you're right Holly. We can't have a bear scaring the children. I'll ask around. Maybe Travis knows someone."

"Hmph," came from Tabitha's direction and then her footsteps sounded leading toward the front of the house.

"Come on ladies, let's finish up here and make sure all the windows and doors are locked," she said. "We wouldn't want a *bear* to break in again. Carol and I are going to use the upstairs rooms for kids games."

"Oh, that will be perfect for the younger kids." Gloria clapped her hands excitedly. "Maggs is going to have an ice skating rink out back and Cindy is setting up the kitchen and dining room for all the baked goods. It will smell so lovely in here."

"I am?"

"Oh definitely," I assured her after seeing the smug look on Tabitha's face. "And we'll have the older kids games outside."

Meredith smiled, "That sounds lovely. Carol and I can do a haunted house in the atrium also. Maybe Travis will help us with that. He said he wanted to be involved."

I smiled back. "That sounds lovely," I repeated.

Not wanting to be left out, Maggs began with, "What about the tu..." she cut off abruptly when I kicked her leg.

"The tubs for the apple bobbing will be fine outside. Thanks for reminding me." Meredith and Carol followed Tabitha into the house.

"What was that for?" Maggs complained as she rubbed her ankle.

I raised my eyebrows at her. "What about keeping the, you know what, secret?" Maggs looked at me sheepishly and shrugged her shoulders.

"Sorry, she just rubs me the wrong way."

"Trust me, we all understand," said Mildred. "Now let's go make a list of supplies." The rest of the afternoon passed uneventfully. The ladies all gave me a list of supplies that needed to be purchased and Carol agreed to help me solicit donations for the raffle. I even had time to schedule a meeting with the estate sale expert at Betty's house. Not a chore I was relishing.

PETE'S FUNERAL

The sun shone brightly through my bedroom window where I was lying, procrastinating getting up. Today was Pete's funeral. I didn't really know him, but as a member of the community and the new chairperson for the festival, I felt it was only right to bid him goodbye.

Thankfully, the funeral was to be held at the community church because it was very cold and windy today. The wind had whistled through the trees outside my window all night, keeping me awake and filling my dreams with ghosts and bears.

The small church on the edge of the lake was beautiful inside. Sunlight shone through the stained glass windows casting different hues across the floor and pews.

At the church, I slipped into a pew next to Vana. She had sold Pete's son, Alex, a house when he'd moved away from home.

"You look terrible."

"Thanks. Barney chased us out of the Blume house yesterday. It was pretty scary."

"Barney?"

"Yes, Barney, the bear."

"You named it?"

"Well, what if there's another one? I need to keep them straight so you know which one I'm talking about."

"Are you anticipating running into another bear?"

"I wasn't anticipating this one. But you never know." The conversation ended as the pastor stepped to the front and began the funeral. The service was a somber one, Pete's son and a few friends speaking about his zest for life and perseverance after breaking both his legs in an accident. He seemed to be a man that never held back at anything.

Soon enough the funeral was over and the people gathered in the church's social hall for a bite to eat. His actual burial would be a private affair with just the immediate family. Conversation filled the air as people took plates of salads and sandwiches, the smell of coffee permeating over everything. I saw Pete's son, Alex, and went up to give my condolences. He was talking to Paul Howard, the optometrist and Pete's best friend.

"It's such a shame about Louella. I just got her new glasses in. She was supposed to pick them up."

"Yes, I heard my dad had been giving her rides into town since she lives just across the street." Alex paused briefly to regain his composure, then smiled, "he would have anyway, even if she had lived all the way across town. That's just the kind of guy he was.

Paul patted Alex's back. "Yes, he was. We lost a good man when we lost your dad. A grumpy man, but a good man." They both laughed together at the truth and Paul walked away. I took my chance and gave Alex a hug.

"I am so sorry, Alex. If there's anything I can do for you, please let me know." When a father dies, there really are no words to console someone.

"Thank you Holly, I really appreciate that. And I appreciate you coming. I know you didn't really know him well." He paused and took a breath and I waited for him to continue. "I gathered a box of his stuff from the previous fall festivals. I thought maybe you could use it. I don't know," his voice trailed off. "He really was a grumpy old guy," he added, smiling.

"I would be happy to look through it. Anything will help, this being my first time and all." I gave him another quick hug and turned to leave when I heard him take a deep breath and clear his throat.

"Uh, Holly?"

"Yes, Alex?"

He bit his lip nervously. "It's just, I'm just wondering." He glanced around quickly. "Would you look into what happened with my dad?" He spoke barely above a whisper. "I think maybe he was murdered."

I stood there frozen in shock. "What..."

"Oh, Alex, I'm so sorry about your father. I turned to see Meredith standing there wearing a tailored black suit. She gave Alex a quick hug. Alex's eyes looked as bewildered as I felt. Did Meredith even know Pete? I frowned back at him.

Meredith stepped back and held Alex at arms length and then it clicked. Was she going after every single man in town?

"That's so kind of you. I wasn't aware you knew my father?" asked Alex confused.

"Oh, no I didn't but I've heard so many kind things said about him since he passed. I feel like I know him."

I rolled my eyes, I couldn't help it and I saw Alex stifle a laugh. "Well thank you Meredith. Holly, perhaps I can talk to you later about selling my father's house. I'll give you a call." He stepped away from Meredith's arms, "I really need to go see to the other guests. Thank you again for coming."

I bit my lip to keep from giggling out loud. Meredith looked a bit put out at being rejected so quickly. A hand on my shoulder made me jump.

"Hey Vana."

"What happened to her," she said, indicating Meredith. I pulled her farther away across the room.

"I'm guessing Alex won't be her next conquest." I really wanted to laugh at her predicament but a funeral is not the best place for that so I settled for biting my lip instead as I watched Alex circulate around the room. I could see why Meredith would be attracted to him. He was very good looking. Even his father in his old age had still been a handsome man.

"What's wrong?" inquired Vana and I realized I was frowning.

Dropping my voice to a whisper I said. "He wants me to look into his father's death." Vana raised her eyebrows at me and took a sip of coffee.

Aloud she said, "I could use a good cup of coffee. Let's go to Katie May's."

"You're drinking coffee."

"I said good coffee." Throwing her cup in the trash we slipped out the door back into the cold. Paul accosted us as we went through the door.

He gave a grimace at the biting wind, snugging his jacket tighter around him. Clouds had moved in and it looked like rain. "Thank you for coming. I know you don't really know him. And thank you for taking over the festival. Pete really loved managing the event. I don't know what he was thinking, spending time in the cold with his legs but he had a bucket list and ice fishing was one of the things on it." He shrugged his shoulders. "Crazy the things people do when they get old."

"I'm sorry for your loss. I heard you and he were good friends."

"Yeah." His eyes got watery so I encouraged him to go home and Vana and I ducked into our cars and cranked up the heat. Thankfully the drive to Katie May's was fairly quick and we hustled inside, where Vana led us to a booth at the back. The delicious scents of breakfast cooking filled the air.

"Why are we sitting here instead of our usual place?"

"I don't want anyone to see us. I have some news."

"What news?"

"I think I know what Alex was talking about." She dropped her voice down low, even though the place was nearly empty. That's how it is in small towns, most of the patrons were probably at Pete's funeral. "Pete wasn't wearing proper clothes to go ice fishing."

I pursed my lips at the news. "Did you also find out how he managed to be frozen into the lake?" The water at the west end of the lake was only a foot deep and froze relatively quickly. It was created specifically to give people a place to ice skate. The east edge dropped down significantly and took till the middle of winter sometimes before it was frozen through. That's why there was a floating barrier at the edge to prevent accidents from happening.

"The coroner thinks he was killed and then placed into the lake before that area froze."

"What?" I exclaimed loudly, then looked around to see if anyone had noticed before continuing on in a whisper. "How did you find out? Nevermind, it was your friend right?"

"I'll never tell. The real mystery is why the police are calling it an accident."

"Unless they know who it is and want them to slip up."

"Why would they do that?"

"Think about it. If the murderer thinks they got away with it, they might slip up. Or the police here are just incompetent. Have you met Detective Moran?"

"Ugh. He's the lead on this case but Travis is assisting. Have you talked to Travis?"

She said it nonchalantly but I knew what she meant. "Not really. I saw him when we found Louella's body." My voice trailed off. Vana is my best friend but how can I tell her how I feel when I don't even know myself? "Have you met Meredith? She seems quite taken with him."

"Just at the funeral just now. Why?"

"Yeeah, she's a different kind of character. Haven't quite put my finger on it but something about her bothers me."

"Besides the hungering after every man in town?"

"You saw that huh? She seems really nice plus she's beautiful and I'm seriously envious of her clothes."

"Speak of the devil."

I turned to see what Vana was looking at and saw Meredith enter the restaurant followed by Travis. There was a sudden pain in my heart as I saw them together. "Does get around," I commented while ducking down behind the menu. Vana followed suit.

"Why are you hiding?" I asked.

"Solidarity."

Katie brought us over a pitcher of coffee and two cups. "You ladies ordering today or just the coffee?" She glanced over to the door. "Oh. How bout I just bring you the French toast combo?" At our nods she put her ticket pad back in her pocket. "I'll seat them on the other side of the room. You can hang onto the menus," she added with a smile. "I can't imagine what he sees in her."

"Are they in here often?" I asked, you know, just out of curiosity.

"A lot. Seen them over at Tipsey's too. Regular gold digger if you ask me. Sorry Holly."

"That's it!" Vana exclaimed loudly and then immediately clamped her hand over her mouth.

Katie winked at her. "That's the way to be subtle. I'll go put your order in." We watched her walk over to Travis and Meredith and seat them at a table across the room and out of direct sight of us.

"She's so awesome," I sighed. "Now what's it?"

"Golddigger. That's what's wrong with her. Plus she's going after your man. Do you think she really solved a crime?"

"Mildred seems to think so." I added sugar and cream to my coffee and gave it a stir. Vana pulled out her phone and punched in some information. "When was the crime and what was it?"

"Hmm, well Mildred said she helped catch some thieves that were targeting the elderly."

Vana tapped on her phone some more. Then made a frowny face at the screen before handing it over to me so I could read the text.

Apparently, Meredith had noticed numerous people entering a building next to hers that was supposed to be vacant and notified the police who then arrested the ring of thieves. I frowned at the screen too. "It hardly seems like she did anything significant," I muttered aloud as I continued reading, then scrolled down the page. "Look at this," I handed the phone back to Vana. "It's a follow up story."

"Oh wow. There was a bank robbery and the former teller, Evelyn Pearce, used to live in that house." She continued to study the screen as Katie brought our breakfasts and left again. I began digging into the French toast, which smelled heavenly. I like to eat it hot with the butter all melty and mixing in with the syrup.

Vana finally looked up and began tucking into her food. "Well, what did it say?" I asked impatiently over a mouthful of bacon and eggs.

"The robbery was over 50 years ago. There couldn't possibly be any connection to the current robberies. The house was most recently used as a meeting place for the Castlemeyer book club until it was condemned."

"Say what?" I choked on my food. "How long ago?"

"It didn't say. Why?"

"Gloria met Meredith at a book club in Castlemeyer. " We stared at each other. The breakfast was momentarily forgotten. Did this have something to do with the break-ins in Appleby? What about the break in at Mildred's? I was going to have to have a chat with Meredith.

"You ladies need more coffee?" Katie's question made us jump. I hadn't even heard her walk up.

I smiled at Katie, "thanks but we're good."

She inclined her head towards Travis and Meredith's table. "Just want to let you know, they aren't being very interesting if you know what I mean," then she went off to help another customer.

"Well that's interesting," Vana said quietly.

"The book club?"

"No. That Katie's looking out for you all of a sudden. You should solve crimes more often."

"Uh, no." I said firmly. "I am not a sleuth."

Vana put down her fork and looked at me seriously. "What do you think you're doing right now?"

"Eating breakfast?"

"You're sleuthing. And, you're enjoying it."

"No. No?" Was I? It made me think. I was just helping out some friends. Is that what sleuthing was, just trying to find answers to help people? "Okay, maybe I am," I finally admitted to her and to myself. "But don't tell people that. I just want to help my friends and the people in town because they are my people. What are you smiling at?"

"You, smiling. You know, I think this sleuthing makes you happy." She raised her eyebrows at me over the rim of her coffee cup. "And we are going to need some more coffee."

A CLUE

It had been an uneventful several days. Pete and Louella were both in the ground, the fall festival plans were proceeding and there had been no more burglaries. I was in the office all morning catching up on work.

The paperwork on the Hotchkiss house had all been finalized and I was just waiting for the transfer to record. MacCready's escrow was proceeding and set to close soon. Joe had been picking up the slack for me as the fall festival plans were taking up a lot of my time but now it was time for lunch and a well deserved break. I shot off a quick text to Meredith, asking if she could meet me for lunch or dinner.

As I exited the office, I nearly ran poor Mildred over. She looked very worried and grabbed my arm to pull me away from the door.

"Oh, Holly. I've got to talk to you, can we go to your office?" She looked around nervously as she spoke barely above a whisper.

Returning to my office, Mildred closed and locked the door, then pulled me onto the couch before speaking again.

"Louella must have called me the morning she died and I guess I missed it. I was playing back my messages and heard this one. You have to hear this."

She put the phone on speaker and played the recording. Louella's voice came over the speaker. "I can't imagine where they might have gotten to. I swear I got into the car with them."

There was silence when presumably someone else was speaking and then, "but I can't see a thing without them. If only my glasses from the optometrist had arrived sooner. I know mine are all scratched, but they're the only ones I've got," then the call ended.

That was it. "Who do you think she was talking to?" asked Mildred.

"What time did this phone call come in?"

Mildred shook her head sadly. "I don't know. It was just in my messages. It doesn't give the date or time. I'm sorry."

I thought for a moment, "Carol told me she got a ride from someone that morning but none of the ladies said they brought her. Who could it have been?"

Mildred just shook her head sadly. "I don't know but I think it was the murderer."

"You what? You think Louella was murdered? Why?"

"I was the first person there at 10:30 and she wasn't around. How early did she get there and why didn't that person stay? Louella would never go walking without her glasses. She was as blind as a bat without them."

I paused to think for a moment and then patted Mildred's hands. "Thank you for bringing this to my attention, Mildred. Now, I'd like to talk to you about the matter from the other day." Mildred pressed her lips together and gave an infinitesimally small nod.

"You knew Betty was living there didn't you?"

She nodded her head some more but kept her eyes on her folded hands in her lap. "She needed someone to bring her supplies," she whispered.

Equally as quietly, I said, "you were using the tunnel to do it. That's why people saw the lights and thought ghosts."

She raised her eyes up to mine suddenly. "We've all made our mistakes, she shouldn't have to suffer for her sister," she exclaimed. "How did you know?"

"After we entered the tunnel, you did nothing but protest us going that way so you must have known what was at the other end." I put my hand over hers. "It's okay. I'm just happy she's alive. Let me walk you back to your store."

"What are you going to do about Louella?"

I smiled. "Apparently I'm a sleuth, so I'm going to do some sleuthing."

After dropping her back at her store, I rang up Travis to pick his brain. I still hadn't heard from Alex, perhaps he had changed his mind. He thought his father had been killed. Mildred thought Louella had been killed. What was going on in this town? There was no evidence that either death was suspicious except, if Louella was looking for her glasses in the car, how did they end up in the weeds? I wonder if Vana's friend could get me a copy of the autopsy report. My phone dinged with a notification reminding me it was time to meet the woman for the estate sale. It was bad enough planning the sale when I thought Betty was dead. Now, I had to go through her things knowing she was alive and pretend she was dead. I left a message for Travis and went to my next appointment.

Louise Belden was a joy and the tiniest woman I had ever met. Her voice tinkled like bells and she radiated happiness. We met on the front porch of Betty's house where she held out her hand to me as I approached.

"Louise Belden at your service."

"Hello Louise, I'm Holly. Thanks for coming all the way out here from Morecroft."

"It's no problem at all. I travel all around the country for my job. You never know what you're going to find." She smiled brightly at me as I let us both into the house.

"Are you always this cheery?"

"I find it's best. You can choose to be happy or not. I choose to be happy."

I smiled at her refreshing attitude. Betty's house was a bit dusty, and the air was stale. As I looked around, it didn't appear that she had taken much, if anything.

"If you don't mind, I'm just going to snoop around and see if there's anything notable then I'll come back later with some staff and price everything. When are you planning on having the sale?"

I hadn't really thought about that aspect of it. "I suppose it should be soon. There's no telling when the bad weather will kick in."

"In that case, I'll plan it for next weekend. That should give me plenty of time to run a notice in the paper."

"Sounds good. Feel free to poke in any nooks you want and I'll do the same." Louise began in the living room and so I wandered off to the rest of the house. There were three bedrooms off the living room, one had clearly been an office. Must be where she wrote her books. I poked into the drawers and the closet but there was no evidence of any book writing, not even a computer. That must have been the one thing she had taken.

In her room, her clothes were still in her drawers, all her medications in the bathroom, and a few pieces of jewelry on the top of the dresser. In the bottom drawer of her dresser I found a small cardboard box with photos and pulled it out. There were a few photos of two girls of various ages which must have been Betty and her sister. My fingers stopped at a photo of four women. One was clearly Betty. Next to her was a stunning woman, then a slim brunette and then. My heart stopped. It was Meredith. I flipped it over and saw that it was dated a few days before the accident.

Had Betty intended on me finding this? Was Meredith here to help Bonnie?

"Holly?" I jumped as Louise spoke my name right behind me. "Oh, I'm sorry, I thought you heard me walk in."

"No, no it's okay. I just found a few photos of Betty. I really miss her." I slipped the photo into my pocket while I spoke.

"I didn't realize you were friends. My company can handle everything if it would be easier."

"I appreciate that, but I'm fine."

"Well I'm done here. Nothing really stands out but everything is in good condition so it should sell well."

"I've put a lock box on the side gate. I can give you a code to use so you can come and go as you please. Oh, and watch out for Jacob up the street, he can be a bit much sometimes." I locked up the house as we walked back through and then left Louise at her car. This was so weird, selling the belongings of someone who was still alive, that just walked away from her life. Actually the last two months had been the weirdest of my life. It made me wonder what could possibly be next.

INTERESTING NEWS

Travis called and asked to meet me by the lake. It was cold out but the wind wasn't blowing so it was tolerable. We were meeting at the bench near where they had found Pete. The tape was still marking off the area, which was weird since we had already buried him.

"Thanks for coming out here. I have to wait for some forensic guys to show up."

"So Pete was murdered?"

He tilted his head to the side and scratched behind his ear. "His son, Alex, came to see me. There were some questions about the way he was found. After what happened last month, the chief thought it best to be thorough."

I nodded my head. "That makes sense. Alex said something to me at the funeral but I haven't heard back from him." Betty said he hated fishing. Paul said it was on his bucket list. Who was right?

"Holly?"

"Mmhmm?"

"You were a million miles away."

"Sorry. Mildred thinks Louella's death is suspicious." Travis sighed and I bit the inside of my cheek to stay quiet.

Instead of commenting, he changed the subject. "I've called animal control about the bear. They're going to have wardens stationed around the event. We can't have it coming back during the festival."

"There wasn't any food in the house so maybe it was just curious," I added.

A breeze blew around the lake and I pulled my coat tighter. I nodded in the direction of the ice rink. "Are they going to open that soon?"

"The parents are already driving me crazy about that but I don't have any control over the forensic investigation. Hopefully it won't be too much longer." He stuffed his hands in his pockets and looked out over the lake. I glanced sideways at him. Even his silhouette was handsome.

I desperately wanted to question what he saw in Meredith. Not that I had any right too, we weren't dating or anything. "So was there anything weird about Pete's death? It seems weird that he would want to go ice fishing before the lake actually froze over." I threw it out there to see if he would bite and he didn't disappoint.

"I'm impressed with how spot on your instincts always are. There's not really any evidence but the scene just feels wrong somehow." I felt him turn towards me. "Do you hang out much with Meredith?"

That was the last thing I expected him to say and it kind of made me angry. I don't know what I was hoping for, but that wasn't it. "Did you really bring me out here to ask me about Meredith? It's pretty cold out here and I should get back to work. Are we done?"

He nodded his head slightly before speaking. "Apparently."

I turned and headed back to my office before he could say anything else. Meredith's sense of timing was impeccable. As I walked away, my phone dinged with a message from her. "Tipsy's at 5?" I answered back with a thumbs up emoji.

Meredith was already seated in a booth when I arrived at 5 p.m. Tipsy's was mostly deserted at this time with only a few people at the bar. The upscale restaurant was dimly lit with accent lighting, an unlit candle sat in the center of the table.

"Holly, I'm so glad you could make some time for me. Everyone speaks so highly of you." Meredith gave me one of her dazzling smiles, her eyes focused intently on me. I could see why men found her so appealing.

"Thank you. I'm looking forward to getting to know you better. I'm sorry, it's taken so long to get together."

Meredith waved her hand in the air. "Oh, it's no problem. Better late than never, right?" she laughed. I took the liberty of ordering us wine, do you mind?"

"Not at all. I could use one right now. It's been a hectic day."

She looked down at her menu, "oh, anything special going on?"

Narrowing my eyes, I hesitated before answering. Something about her actions seemed deliberate. Then I shook my head no as I said, "not really, just the festival coming up has really seemed to take up a lot of my time lately and real estate is always something else."

She placed the menu carefully on the table. "I can imagine. So what's good here?"

"Everything here is good but I really love the chicken parmesan."

"Sounds great." The waitress came and took our orders and brought two glasses of red wine, a perfect choice to accompany our dinner.

I swirled the wine in my glass before taking a sip. The sweet notes danced on my taste buds. "Mm, this is perfect. How are you liking our little town?" I asked.

"It's great. The people are great."

"So you met Gloria and Mildred in Castlemeyer at a book club? How long have you known them?"

Mildred twisted the stem of the wine glass between her fingers while she answered. "The book club disbanded about six years ago. The building was condemned. But Gloria and Mildred and I have stayed in touch through social media groups."

"Mildred is on social media?" I asked surprised, although I guess I shouldn't be. The internet has been around for a good long time now.

"Oh yes. She's a whiz at the computer. Gloria too."

"So, tell me more about this crime you helped solve." I prodded her.

"Well, not much to say. I live next door to the building. It's actually kind of an eyesore now. I was hearing noises and one night I saw a flashlight inside. I just thought it was kids, you know, so I went over the next day to have a look around and found boards pried off the walls and the floor." She shrugged as if it was nothing.

"So you called the police?"

"Um, yes. I mean, what if they came to my house next? I've been advocating for them tearing that building down for years but the city council won't do anything about it."

"So what were they looking for?"

"Huh?"

"The kids. They must have been looking for something right?"

"Who knows with kids." She shook her head sadly. "Parents just don't raise their kids right anymore. They let them run around without supervision. It's sad really."

Now I was really confused. That's all she did, make a phone call? "Did you hear about the break-ins here?"

"Oh yes, Travis told me all about them." He did?

"You don't suppose they are connected to the break-ins in Castlemeyer do you?"

Meredith froze for a second before answering. It was quick but I know what I saw. She settled back into the seat. "I doubt it. Travis thinks it's just thieves looking for something easy to steal, money, watches, things like that. That's why people should lock up their valuables. I always do." Her right hand fiddled with the silverware, then glanced over my shoulder.

The waitress set our plates of steamy goodness on the table. The breaded chicken was light and crispy and smelled heavenly. "Can I get you anything else?"

"No, thanks. This looks great." I tucked in as she walked away. I couldn't resist the deliciousness sitting in front of me.

"You're right. This food is the best. Who knew a little restaurant like this could produce something this good."

The next few minutes went by in silence except for the sound of chewing. I was twirling spaghetti on my fork when Meredith spoke next.

"I wanted to let you know that Travis and I have been spending time together," she spoke quietly but I inferred the question.

I chewed the bite of spaghetti slowly, then swallowed and washed it down with a sip of wine. "That's nice. I'm glad you two are getting along." I twirled some more spaghetti slowly.

Meredith leaned forward on the table. "It's just people have been saying that you two were..."

I cut her off. "No, more like I was interfering in his investigation," I joked. "You know how cops are with their proprietary information."

Meredith sighed in relief. "Okay. I just wanted to make sure. I really like you Holly. I didn't want to interfere in something you might have going on."

Giving her a smile I didn't feel, I sealed the deal. "No, we don't have anything going on. My husband, Evan, died in a car accident ten years ago and I guess I'm just not ready for dating yet."

"I'm so sorry Holly."

I decided to go for the gut punch, "Yes, it was a drunk driver. The front passenger died also and two other passengers were injured. One of them was Travis's wife. Honestly, drunk people should be put away for life." I tucked the forkful of spaghetti into my mouth.

Meredith's hand stilled on the table. My heart was racing as I waited for a reaction but I forced myself to breathe normally while I chewed my food. I picked up my knife and began slicing my chicken into small pieces.

"That's terrible. I agree about drunk drivers. They shouldn't get a second chance." Something in her tone alarmed me.

BOOK CLUB

I was going to need some help if I was going to get to the bottom of this and still run my business so I invited Mildred, Gloria, Cindy and Maggs to my house for brunch. I made tea and picked up some pastries from the bakery. After everyone was seated and had something to eat and drink I began with my plan.

"Ladies, you said you used to belong to a book club and I thought you might want to begin one here."

Gloria looked a little doubtful. "What kind of a book club?"

"A mystery book club. Without the books."

"Say what? How can that be a book club? Oh." It took a moment for Maggs but it finally sank in. "You want us to be a part of a murder mystery club."

I shrugged. "You could call it that."

"I am calling it that."

"I just thought it might be better if it was a 'book' club so no one knows we're investigating."

Cindy raised her hand. "You don't need to raise your hand Cindy."

"What if someone else wants to join?"

We all looked at each other for a moment. Dang the idea had seemed so brilliant.

"That's okay dear," said Mildred. "They can just start their own."

Well that works. "Okay ladies. It seems there is some suspicion surrounding Pete's death and possibly Louella's. Now I don't want you ladies snooping and getting into trouble, but if you happen to overhear anything interesting, you can bring it back to the group and we'll go over it."

Mildred was fidgeting in her chair as I continued on. "Now everyone must swear not to discuss anything outside of the group. What happens during book club stays in book club."

Gloria giggled. "That sounds like the line from that fight club movie."

"Where do you think I got it from? A friend once told me not to reinvent the wheel."

Cindy raised her hand. "Cindy, if you raise your hand again, I'm going to throw something at it." She grimaced and ducked it back down into her lap.

"It's just, I was talking to Charlie. You know, Louella's son, and he told me that Pete had been giving her rides into town and I just wondered." She floundered a bit before continuing. "Do you think there's something in that? I mean, they both ride together and now they're both..." she ran her finger across her throat.

My eyebrows climbed up my forehead. I had kind of associated Cindy with Betty White and that movement just cinched it for me.

"And thank you for including me. I tend to get overlooked a lot." It was probably her polite demeanor that led people to do that but I could see she was a smart cookie.

"I wouldn't want anyone else but you Cindy." Mildred was still looking agitated in her seat. What could possibly be wrong with her? "Mildred, are you okay?" The ladies all turned their heads to look at her.

"It's not my place to say this. I promised I wouldn't." She twisted her hands together in her lap. "No. I shouldn't."

"Just say it!" we all yelled at once.

"Since everything here is a secret, it is a secret right ladies?"

"Yes!"

Her next words came out in a rush leaving everyone shocked and speechless. "Betty is still alive. She faked her death to get away from her sister and I've been sneaking supplies to her through the tunnel in the Blume house." She heaved a deep sigh after her impromptu speech.

Everyone looked at her with big round eyes and open mouths.

"I'm sorry, I just can't do it by myself anymore. Now you can all help. With the festival there I'm afraid it will get found out."

Maggs was the first to get it together. "Now Mildred, how could you get us involved with something like this. Of course we'll help out, but really." She looked at her with a stern face.

"Oh please, Maggs. You really need to stop framing everything as a complaint first," I admonished her. "You were wonderful leading us in the cave and I think you might actually enjoy this."

"Oh you were," gushed Gloria. "This is so exciting."

I took advantage of the moment to pop a pastry in my mouth which was exactly when Carol asked me a question. "So when do we start?" All eyes turned to me and my stuffed mouth as I tried to choke it down so I could speak.

Finally swallowing the last bite I began. "I've a few things. To start with, Mildred received a call from Louella that had her searching for her glasses in someone's car, but I found them in the weeds outside Blume house. How did they get there? Who dropped her off at the house?"

"Oh, we should start a murder board," interrupted Cindy.

"A what?" I asked.

"You know, a board that we put the pictures of suspects on and notes to keep everything straight," Maggs explained.

I went searching for a pen and paper as I talked. I found what I wanted in the junk drawer and sat back down. "I don't have anything like that here but I've got paper and a pen." I wrote down the first questions. "Does anyone else have anything?"

Cindy began to raise her hand then dropped it when she caught my eye. "Gloria was with Meredith when she found Pete." She turned to look at Gloria. "Didn't you say it was weird about Pete's clothes?"

Gloria pressed her lips together. "Yes. He was wearing a 30 degree jacket but it had no wool lining. There's no way a man his age would have gone out there wearing that. Plus, his legs had to be hurting him."

"Paul said ice fishing was on his bucket list but Betty said he hated fishing," I said.

"Plus it wasn't frozen yet. The lake. It didn't freeze until early the next morning. Maybe someone killed him and threw him in the lake after he was dead." Cindy leaned forward as she was speaking and selected another pastry and then settled back into the couch to enjoy it.

Maggs suddenly sat up straight. "Maybe it's the thieves. You know, the ones that have been robbing vacant houses." She turned to Mildred. "Didn't they break into your house too?"

"It was just the one guy and he got arrested." She suddenly looked concerned. "Are the break-ins still happening?"

Maggs raised her eyes and cocked her head to the side in a knowing way. "Meredith said they are."

Meredith again. She sure has her fingers poked in every pie.

"Is something wrong Holly?" asked Mildred.

"Travis has been seeing Meredith," popped in Gloria.

I shook my head. "It's not that. It just seems like Meredith is everywhere lately. You said she found Pete?" The ladies nodded their heads. How had I missed that information. "She found Louella too."

I turned to look at Gloria, "How did you guys find her? I had to lean over the side to see her and nearly fell to my death."

She shook her head and shrugged her shoulders. "It was Meredith who pointed her out. Of course, she is taller than me. Perhaps she could see better."

Hmm, what could she possibly have seen. Maybe I could talk to Joanna. She was the receptionist at the police station. She'd given me inside information before.

"Does anyone have anything else?" Four heads shook back and forth. "Why don't we all coordinate supply runs with Mildred for you know who. We can meet here on Monday unless someone finds out some really good news.

"I'll bring the murder board," chimed in Carol.

OPPORTUNITIES

My whole next day was taken up with work. Sending out mailers, finalizing files, and tracking down leads on new buyers and sellers. The winter bunnies were just beginning to arrive for the festival. Skiing should begin soon, although we had yet to receive our first snowfall.

A knock at the door had me pop my head up from the computer in time to see Joe poke his head around.

"Joe, why are you knocking?"

"Hi Holly, can we talk?" Uh oh. This can't be good.

"Sure thing, come in." I smiled at him, warmly I hoped. He'd put me in a bit of a pickle when he sided with Bonnie against me but I held that more against her than him. "I wanted to tell you how great you're doing. You're not quitting on me are you? Do you need a raise?"

Better to head it off and let him know his options than to have to hire a new assistant. It takes so long to break them in.

Joe settled himself on the couch before broaching the subject. "No. I'm not quitting. I really like working for you and I really appreciate you giving me my job back." He took a deep breath. "I would like to get my own license. I think I can help you out more if I have one. What do you think?"

He's right, he could do more if he was licensed. As I thought about it I realized he could do so much more. He could show houses and assist with the open houses, fill out contracts. "I think that's a wonderful idea. If you need any help with anything let me know."

He fidgeted a bit. "That's the thing. I don't really have the money for the classes. If you could front it for me, I could pay you back."

I waved my hand to cut him off. "Don't say another word. Of course, I will and you don't have to pay me back. Consider it a perk for being my assistant. Just study hard and pass the test."

He breathed a sigh of relief. "Thank you Holly. I really don't deserve any of the stuff you have done for me after what I did."

"That's the past Joe. I don't want to talk about it anymore. Today is a new day and a new beginning and that's what we should focus on. "Did you get the signed listing back on Betty's house?"

"Yes, and I've already scheduled the sign to go up."

"Thanks. I met with Louise, the appraiser for the estate sale. She's awesome. We're having the sale next weekend. I don't imagine there's too much of value, but you never know."

We settled into our normal rhythm of work and it made me feel contented having something familiar and reliable to focus on.

Vana and Lucy dropped by the office in the afternoon and I filled them in on the updates. Of course I didn't mention the 'book club' because a promise had been made and if I made an exception, others would too. It did make me feel conflicted though. After I finished my spiel, we sat looking at each other.

"That's interesting. I guess you've committed to the sleuthing then?" inquired Vana.

"Uh, the what?" asked a puzzled Lucy.

"Holly has finally realized that she likes solving puzzles."

I held up my forefinger, "you mean helping people and, I think maybe I should start dating." I began to chew on that self same finger. Both ladies looked surprised.

"Are you going to start with Travis?" inquired Lucy who for some reason suddenly needed to study her fingernails.

"He seems to be interested in Meredith and I'm not interested in anyone who's interested in someone else. So, no."

A big smile creased Vana's face. "No." I said firmly. "I will find them myself or maybe Lucy has a suggestion?"

Lucy rubbed her hands together. "Oh, this is so exciting. Sorry Vana." Lucy shot her a commiserating look but just barely before the grin hit her face again sparking worry on my own. Had I created a monster?

"Don't look so worried," she said consolingly, this is going to be great."

Vana gave us both her 'mom' look. "You two are just like every movie where the girl dates all the wrong people before realizing the right one was there all the time."

Frowning, I said. "This isn't a movie. It's real life. My life. And I get to choose."

CHLOE TIME

I woke up the next morning in high spirits. Today was my day to spend with my granddaughter Chloe. My daughter Penelope had been calling unexpectedly to have me watch her lately and it had begun to interfere with my work schedule, which, although it is adjustable, I needed to set some boundaries.

So after the whole murder investigations shenanigans from last month, I had laid down the law and now have a regular day each week to spend with Chloe. It might vary, but I always know in advance now. She is only four and still excited by everything. Penelope dropped her off at 8 a.m. so she could get to work and I welcomed Chloe into my warm house with a big hug and Ginger added a kiss on her way through the door, nearly making her drop her bundle of blankie and dolls.

"Can we go for a walk grandma?"

"Of course. Why don't we make some cookies first and take them to our neighbor Ben to thank him for fixing my fence? He has the cutest dog, named Bernard."

"Can Ginger come?"

"Of course, honey." Chloe didn't care that I was cheating with pre-made cookie dough. She just enjoyed making them with her grandma and eating a few fresh from the oven. After they cooled, I bundled them up onto a paper plate which I then slid into a freezer bag so Ginger wouldn't spill them with her boisterousness.

It was nearly ten o'clock before we were ready to go. I bundled Chloe and myself up in jackets, scarves and gloves before setting out. It was a beautiful crisp and clear but cold day. Ben was excited to see us, Ginger even more so. We spent a few minutes talking to him and giving him the cookies before taking our leave and continuing on down the road.

We were just passing Mildred's house when she called out to us, greeting us with a big smile. "Hello ladies. How are you two doing this fine morning?"

"We gave Ben some cookies. He helped me escape proof my backyard so Ginger can't get out." At the mention of her name, Ginger flicked up her ears. I think she was a little perturbed at not getting a cookie.

Mildred laughed. "Yes, he told me about that." Then she looked serious. "How is she going to protect us, if she can't get out?" Ginger whined and looked up at me as if to say, 'see?'

"It's for your protection Ginger. There are bears out there. Chloe, why don't you and Ginger go look at Mildred's flowers?" I pushed the two of them through her gate and closed it behind me.

"How's the investigation going on the robberies?" I spoke quietly as I didn't want to worry Chloe.

Mildred shrugged her shoulders. "The man they arrested is keeping mum and they don't seem to have any other leads."

"That's a shame," I paused to watch Chloe and Ginger prance around the garden. Mildred put her hand on my arm.

"You shouldn't be too hard on Meredith. Even as a young girl, she always wanted to be the center of attention. Once you know that, it's easier to handle her."

"Hmph, I guess so. Wait, you lived in Castlemeyer?"

"Oh it was so long ago. That's where I met my husband. We moved here when we retired."

"I had no idea. Of course I've only lived here for ten years but it feels like a lifetime." Mildred shivered and I suddenly felt bad. Here I was talking and the poor lady was freezing. "You should get inside, I need to get Chloe home anyway."

Together, Chloe, Ginger and I walked home and then spent the rest of the afternoon, watching cartoons and playing board games.

Alex finally gave me a call late that evening after Chloe had gone home. "Hello Alex, I was wondering if you were going to call."

"Hi Holly. I'm sorry, it took me so long. I was going through my dad's things and…" There was a long break, then he began again in a softer voice. "I'm going to miss him so much."

"I'm really sorry, Alex. Just let me know what I can do for you."

There was a little sniffle and I could hear the tears in his voice over the line. "If you could list the house that would be great. Miss Belmar keeps bugging me about listing. I just want her off my back."

"Of course, that won't be any problem, I can bring over the papers in the morning and get a sign up first thing. Do you need any help going through your father's things? I would be more than happy to help."

"Thanks Holly. I want to say no, but I think…I'm sorry, this has been harder on me than I thought. I mean, I know he was old, but it was so unexpected. Would you mind?"

"Of course not, Alex. I do understand what it feels like to lose someone so unexpectedly. Does 9 a.m. work for you?"

"Yes. Thanks again Holly. You really are as nice and kind as people say."

"Well, thank you Alex. Now try and get some sleep and I'll see you tomorrow." And then I can ask him about why he thinks his father was murdered.

CLUES

It's 1 a.m. and I can't sleep. I lay in the pitch black darkness of my bedroom, not sleeping. Knowing it was totally the wrong thing to do, I turned on my phone and began scrolling through it. Curiosity overcame me and I googled Meredith's name. The same story Vana had found popped up and I reread it. Going back to the search page, I found more of the same story with slight variations.

With a little trepidation, I looked up the story of my husband's accident but found all the same stories my sister had already saved for me from the newspapers. What she hadn't been able to save was an electronic obituary notice. I clicked on it and found a section where people were able to leave, I guess you would call it, sympathy notes.

Reading through them made me feel the pang of his loss all over again, 'what a wonderful man,' 'so kind,' but I knew all that, he had been a wonderful husband and father. As I read the next one, a chill began to spread through my body. Had someone made a mistake? It said, "Don't worry love, all wrongs will be avenged." What could that possibly mean? It was only signed, Meri. I couldn't recall us knowing anyone named Meri.

It must be a mistake. Things happen, especially with electronics. Putting it out of my mind, I scrolled back to the articles. There was one writer who had given updates on the accident, a Joanna Aguirre, I resolved to call her in the morning. Maybe she had some behind the scenes info she would share with me. She would know if Meredith was the fourth girl in the car.

I WOKE EARLY THE NEXT morning, tired after a restless night, and after a quick breakfast for both Ginger and myself, I left the house with my camera and a desire for some answers. Pete lived in the center of town and between his house and mine was the Blume house and the lake and I intended on looking at both of the death scenes.

Although I had met Travis near the sight of Pete's demise, I hadn't really gotten a chance to look around. Policemen could be so touchy when it came to crime scenes. First though, I drove up the hill to the Blume house. The sun was barely cresting the top of the mountain when I arrived and the house was still shrouded in shadows.

I sat staring at it through my windshield, examining the windows for any sign of movement. Did that curtain on the second floor twitch? Holly get a hold of yourself. Exiting the car, I walked briskly along the path that led to the cliff where Louella had fallen. Poor woman. Sure she was old, but what a terrible way to go. It was eerily quiet, not even the birds were singing. Was the house really haunted?

Emerging from the shadows of the trees, the view was exhilarating. The whole valley of trees spread out before me and just then, the sunlight hit the lake surface creating thousands of sparkling diamonds.

There really was something magical in the early morning light. Tearing my eyes away from the view, I scanned the ground near the area where Louella had fallen, or was pushed, while my ears listened for any strange noises. If she had been killed, I didn't want to become another victim. What would link the two of them, Pete and Louella? She didn't have her glasses, I found them, but she was looking for them in a car? And who's car was it? Alex said his dad had been giving her rides but he was dead by then.

I finally found the spot where my foot had slipped when I looked for Louella. How could Meredith possibly have found her? Sure her arm had been sticking out of the bush but still. I laid down on my belly and peered over the edge. The bushes in the area where Louella had been were all trampled down. A twig snapped and I slid back and jumped to my feet.

Apparently, those karate classes were beginning to do me some good.

"Who's there?" I called to the silent woods. Fearing Barney had come back, and at the same time relieved that maybe it was just the bear, I brushed the detritus off my clothes and hurried back to my car, not stopping until I was safely inside with the engine running and the doors locked.

I put the car in drive, eager to be any place but here. My car lurched forward sluggishly. Well, that can't be good. Putting my car in park I left it running and got out to survey my tires, hoping I was just stuck in a hole. I wasn't. My right rear tire was flat. I must have run over a nail or something in the drive. Honestly, with a house as old as the Blume house, I'm surprised it didn't happen sooner.

Thankful I was wearing pants and flat shoes today, I took out the jack and spare and set about changing the tire, taking frequent glances around to ensure Barney wasn't around. As a single mom, I learned a long time ago how to do basic maintenance on my car including changing a flat. Less than 20 minutes later, I was good to go and proud that I could still change it quickly. The most difficult part was always loosening the lug nuts. My secret is to use a four way lug wrench and step on the bar to turn it. Works like a charm every time.

It's a little known fact that there's an angel and a devil sitting on your shoulders and guiding your choices. Safely ensconced in my car once again, and on my way down the mountain to the location of Pete's demise, these two had an argument over how Louella had fallen.

Devil: You know it was Meredith AND she's trying to steal your guy.

Angel: It could have been Meredith but why?

Devil: She probably killed Pete too.

Angel: Again, why? Just because you don't like the woman doesn't mean she's a murderer.

Devil: Maybe she needs a good push over the cliff.

That thought made me pause. My foot definitely slipped in the dirt. Where was the mark from Louella slipping? If she had been pushed, there wouldn't be a mark. Why did she get there so much earlier than the rest of us? It wasn't to take a walk because she couldn't find her glasses when she got out of the car. How did they get in the weeds? They had to be in the car when she got dropped off, otherwise, I wouldn't have found them by the house.

By this time, I had meandered my way down the twisting mountain roads, completely missing all the beauty of the early morning forest. I pulled into the parking lot at my office, locked my car and hurried over to the lake.

The police tape had all been removed and the only sign any tragedy had occurred there were the small bundles of flowers and candles left by well-wishers. The east side of the lake was frozen completely over where the ice skating was held. From there it dropped off dramatically and only a few feet around the edge was frozen over. A barrier prevented the skaters from going beyond the designated frozen part.

Now that's strange. The part where the police tape had been was only frozen two feet out. Nobody would ice fish there. Not that I ice fished, but I had only ever seen them out near the deeper water. Was he pretending to ice fish to get it off his bucket list? Was he ill? Then I remembered Gloria complaining about her hip hurting in the cold. Pete had two metal rods in his legs, wouldn't that have caused him pain in the cold?

The more I thought about it, the more convinced I became that Pete's death was not natural. I definitely needed to ask Alex why he was suspicious. Back at my office, I printed out the listing agreement for Alex to sign as well as some disclosures, and then popped back into my car for the short drive to his house mentally reminding myself to get my tire replaced on the way back.

ALEX

Pete had lived in an older wood frame house with a peaked roof, typical of homes in the area. Alex let me into a cozy living room with a fire roaring in the wood burning stove. Many people opted for these over a fireplace in their mountain homes because it heated better and you could use it all night. A very handy thing in these colder winter months.

"Thanks for coming by Holly, I really appreciate it. Oh and before I forget, here's the box of files from the past fall festivals."

"Thank you Alex. I'm sure it will be very useful, especially for collecting donations for the raffle. How are you doing?"

Alex ran his fingers through his sandy hair. "I'll admit, it's been tougher than I thought especially when..." his words ran out and I filled in what I thought he was going to say.

"Especially if he was murdered." I let the word hang in the air and waited for him to respond.

He gave a quick nod and then shook his head. "I feel like he got cheated. Why did someone steal that time away from him?" His voice trembled and his eyes watered. I gave him a quick hug.

"Why don't we sit down and talk. I brought the paperwork for you to sign. If that's what you want to do." He followed me to the couch and sat across from me.

Alex swallowed a few times and looked around at the cozy room. I followed his gaze. There were old west paintings on the wall and the fireplace tools had horse heads on them. "Your dad seemed to like the old west."

"Uh, yes. When he was younger, he worked on a horse ranch. That's how he broke his legs. His horse slipped on a hill and rolled over him. It was pretty bad, took him nearly a year to walk again." He smiled at the memory. "My dad never gave up. He was a real fighter."

I placed my hand on his knee. "I'm so very sorry. It's never easy losing someone you love." Taking a deep breath I plunged on. "Alex, why do you think he was killed?"

He bit his lip to keep it from trembling and then anger overtook him. "Three reasons. My dad hated fishing. The cold always made his legs ache and Louella."

"What about Louella?"

"My dad was giving her rides around town. One of her grandkids had sat on her glasses while going down the slide." He threw his hands up in the air. "I know, I know. I didn't believe it either, but the little bugger did it. His mom saw him. My dad dies and then a few days later Louella accidentally 'falls.'" He put finger quotes around accidentally when he said it. "I don't believe it. I saw her glasses, they were toast." His anger petered out.

"I don't believe it either."

"Then you believe me?" he asked hopefully. "Detective Moran didn't believe me."

Smiling, I said, "Yes, I do. I think the police have to be a little skeptical but there's just too many things bothering me. Do you have any idea who might have done it?"

Shaking his head no, a tear leaked down his cheek. "Help me."

I patted his knee again. "I'm already working on it. After he composed himself, he showed me the house and I snapped a few pictures, before having him sign the listing agreement. He already owned another home and wasn't interested in renting the place but I gave him all the options. I wanted to be sure that he wouldn't regret his decision later.

A tire replacement later and I was back at my office going through the box which turned out to be a treasure trove of patrons who made donations every year. I decided to turn it over to Joe to make donation calls. The fall festival was only a week away and he would have the time to make this a priority. I also gave him the number for Carol so they could coordinate.

I was totally engrossed in my work and a knock at the door made me jump. "Come in, " I called wondering who it was because most people just walked right on in. I was surprised to see it was my daughter Penelope.

"Hi mom. I was wondering if you could go to lunch?" Penelope was 24 and had the same slim figure and sandy hair as her father. After he died, it was both painful and comforting to see him reflected in her.

"I could," I replied wondering what she was up to. Unfortunately, she can also read me like a book.

"You don't have to be suspicious mom," she laughed. "I just wanted to treat you."

"Well, then, of course I can. I'm always up for a free lunch."

We passed Omar waiting on the printer on our way out. "Did you get an offer?" I asked.

He looked up frowning. "What? Oh yes, thank you."

"Is everything okay? You were frowning."

"Oh heah, just fine. Just business. Everything okay with the car?"

"Yup, my daughter is taking me to lunch. Good luck with your offer."

The cold air hit us as soon as we opened the door. "What's wrong with your car?" Penelope asked me with concern.

"Nothing, I had some problems a few weeks ago. Omar used to be a mechanic. Oh, and I had a flat today. You will be proud of your old mom. I changed it all by myself."

"Way to go mom!"

We walked the short block over to Katie May's. The cold air was refreshing. Odd how you can smell the different seasons in the air and I inhaled the autumn scents deeply.

"Mom, I just wanted to say thank you for pointing out to me that I needed to get organized. I have been winging it and it wasn't fair to you or Chloe. She is so much more settled now and she gets so excited when it's time to go to your house every week."

"I'm glad my pushing helped you. That's what us moms do. And you know? It's helped me get more organized also."

"You more organized? You're the most organized person I know."

"Maybe. I think I wing it a little too much." I sighed. "Maybe that's where you get it from. All I know is, I really like having my time planned. Being flexible can be a good thing but somewhere along the line it kind of got out of hand."

Penelope smiled. "I'm glad we both got benefits out of this."

Warm air enveloped us lke a blanket as we pushed open the door to Katie May'. The place was bustling with people for lunch. Bits of conversation floated through the air along with the smell of coffee and chicken soup. People were starting to gravitate toward the hearty winter meals from sandwiches and Katie May was always happy to oblige. Penelope and I found a booth near the back and settled in. I ordered us two ice teas while Penelope went to use the restroom. She looked a little unsettled when she returned.

"That horrible Bonnie is sitting by the bathroom. How can she even show her face in public?"

"Because she's horrible. Who is she with?"

"I don't know, some woman who looks like she stepped out of a designer magazine."

My heart froze. "Brunette hair and thin?"

"Yeah, how did you know?"

That could only be Meredith. What was she doing with Bonnie? I smiled at my daughter to reassure her. "She's just a woman I met recently. Maybe she's doing business with her." I leaned over the table and patted Penelope's hand. "Don't worry about her. I'm not going to let her ruin one more moment of my life."

"But mom."

"No. Now, what is my daughter going to buy me for lunch today?"

I enjoyed the most wonderful time with my daughter that I've had in years that afternoon. Amazing that setting one little boundary would make all the difference in the world. Perhaps it was now time for me to reevaluate all my life choices. Nah, who am I kidding. I like the me I've become. I realized I was smiling to myself as I drove home later that afternoon.

FASCINATING FACTS

B iting the nails on my left hand, I dialed the number for the Morecroft Tribune with the other hand. After two rings, the phone was answered by a pleasant voice.

"Morecroft Tribune. How may I direct your call?"

"Hello, I'm looking for Joanna Aguirre? Does she still work there?" I kicked myself for not checking this before I called.

"Just a moment please."

After an interminable period of horrible elevator music, a voice came back on the line. "Hello, this is Joanna. How can I help you?"

"Hello, this is Holly Holcraft, I'm a real estate agent, not that that has anything to do with why I called." Great, now she's going to think I'm a lunatic. I took a breath and began again. "I'm sorry. Let me start over. You wrote about my husband's car accident ten years ago, an Evan Holcraft? I'm sorry, I wasn't really expecting you to still be there. I'm sorry." Ugh. I decided to shut up before I put my foot even further in my mouth. Hopefully, she received worse calls.

"Yes, I did. Are you his wife?"

"Yes."

"Oh, I'm so sorry."

"It's okay, it was a long time ago," I said apologetically.

"No. I mean I'm sorry for what I have to tell you. I wanted to call you so many times over the years but it just didn't seem right to cause you more pain when you were grieving. We're not all heartless reporters."

Wait, what? "I found a picture with four women in it from just before the crash. Was the fourth woman in the car named Meredith Maroney? There was never a name."

"Look Holly, I'm, I've got a deadline to meet. Can I see you in person? I'll come to you and bring all my notes and we can talk. Monday morning?"

"Sure, how about Katie Mays in town. Mondays are usually pretty slow." We finalized the time and she hung up. A cold prickling fear began creeping up my spine.

UNEXPECTED NEWS

I t was only a few days until the fall festival and everyone in town was excited. Joe had done a fabulous job of lining up donors for the event thanks to Pete's meticulous notes. The ladies had most of their booths ready to go and tickets were selling like hotcakes. My job today was to go around and pick up donations for the raffle from the local businesses. My first stop today would be Mildred's candy store.

A steady rain had fallen all morning so I bundled up warmly and brought along my rain boots just in case. My phone rang just as I was ready to set out. The caller ID showed the call came from city hall so I answered with my most professional voice.

"Hello, this is Holly Holcraft, how can I help you?"

"Good morning Holly. This is Mayor Townsend," his cheery voice came over the line. "Would it be possible for you to swing by my office this morning?"

"Of course. I was just getting ready to leave. I'll be there in a few minutes." Mildred would have to wait. City Hall was only a few blocks away butted up against the mountain to the south of town. It took longer to bundle myself into the car with my jacket, gloves and scarf on, then it did to drive the few blocks to get there.

Once inside, I peeled off the accessories on my way through the marble lobby lined with portraits of past mayors and presented myself to the Mayor's secretary. Alda Montgomery always looked put together in a way I strived to manage but failed most days. She was always the utmost professional but today she seemed a little agitated and looked at me with sympathy. "I'll let the Mayor know you're here."

She knocked on the door and then motioned me to go inside where I stopped floored by the sight of the woman sitting in front of the Mayor's desk. Mayor Townsend rose from his chair and hurried around the desk to greet me.

"Thank you for coming Holly. I believe you know Bonnie Belmar. The City Council has just hired her to manage all the festivals throughout the year." I watched in shock as Bonnie turned her face towards me with a smug smile plastered across it.

"Oh, we know each other," she said in a sickly sweet voice. "I'm so delighted to be working with you again, Holly."

The Mayor returned to his seat behind the desk. "I'm glad to hear that. I just know the two of you will get along well together, both of you being in real estate should be a real asset with all of the people you know. From now on, just keep Bonnie in the loop on all your preparations for the festival." He continued to ramble on oblivious to the animosity between us.

I plastered a fake smile across my face as well. "Thank you for letting me know, Mayor Townsend. I'll be sure to do that. If there's nothing else, I've got to be running along, so many things still to do with the festival."

"Of course you do. Thank you so much for taking on this job. I really appreciate it." Somehow I managed to remove myself without causing a scene. As I passed Alda's desk, she mouthed 'sorry' at me and I nodded at her as I walked by.

I felt nauseous. How am I going to report to her of all people. Part of this situation was my own fault. Most people didn't know that Bonnie was responsible for killing my husband because she was driving drunk. I'm not the type of person that drags out people's dirty laundry for all to see and part of me now regretted that decision. Maybe I could have Joe act as a go between I mean that's what real estate is all about. My client talks to me and I talk to the other agent and that agent talks to their client who then tells their agent what they want, who tells me etc.. It's like playing telephone, adult telephone. Yes, definitely, Joe would be my insulation between me and her. Besides, he owed me big time. It was just this one festival and in a few days it would all be over. If Bonnie hoped to stick it to me, then she should have started sooner. Ha! Take that Bonnie. I thrust an imaginary spear through my nemesis and then proceeded to continue on with my day as if the meeting had never happened. But peace was not to be had.

THE CANDY STORE

The door to Mildred's candy shop tinkled as I stepped into the store. I always loved the candy store because it reminded me of the scent of a bucket full of Halloween candy, all those delicious flavors all mingled together. The pleasantness lasted all of two seconds until I saw Travis standing in front of the counter speaking with Mildred.

"Oh, Holly hello. The detective here is just following up on that nastiness from the other day. I've got your basket here all ready to go." She came around the counter with a huge basket filled with goodies and wrapped in cellophane. "I do hope you like it."

"Wow, Mildred, this is amazing. It's perfect for the raffle. I might even bid on it myself."

Travis cleared his throat. "You might have a little competition."

"Hello detective. How's the break-in investigation going?" I asked lightly. "Catch anymore crooks?" It was hard to avoid admiring all six foot two of his handsomeness. Dang, I really need to go on a date with anyone else. Travis held too much baggage for me.

Travis smiled and it lit up his face. "Hi Holly. Good to see you." His smile faded and he became serious. "We don't have very many leads. The intruder from Mildred's isn't speaking. It's kind of weird actually. Usually petty crooks turn on each other in an instant." He shrugged.

"Would you two mind the shop for me for a moment? I need to run to the loo. Thanks so much." Mildred smiled and hurried off but I knew what she was up to.

"Holly," began Travis but I held my hand up to stop him.

"Let the man speak," yelled Mildred from the back room and I blushed. Perhaps I should let him talk but I was afraid of what he would say.

"Holly. I'm sorry about the way you found out. I really did try to tell you. Do you think we could be friends? We're going to keep running into each other and I think you know, it's awkward." Okay, that was not it.

His use of the word friend cut me like a knife and why was that? It's not like I wanted to date him. I just didn't want Meredith to be dating him. I realized he was still waiting for an answer.

"I will admit it is a bit awkward. I'm not mad at you, I'm really not." I pressed my lips together in a thin line and then rubbed my face with my hands. "I thought I had processed Evan's death but..." I bit my lip as my words failed me.

"It's okay. I understand." Travis held out his hand. "Friends?"

I smiled briefly as I shook it. "Sure." His hand was warm and strong and it bothered me that I thought that. Guilt panged through me.

"How was that escape room? Lucy told me you got locked in?"

"Yeah, that was an experience," I laughed. "I'm still not sure which room was the first room. If you go, let me know."

"Sure thing. I was thinking of taking Meredith there."

You what? Instead of making a smart remark I nonchalantly said, "Oh. Are you two dating?"

Before answering Travis gave me the most intense look. "We've gone a few places. She's uh, different."

"Huh. Well, I should get going. Work to do and stuff. Lots of stuff." I grabbed the basket of goodies and backed out the door before he could speak. I seemed to be doing that a lot lately. Our eyes met for a heart stopping moment and I felt like he wanted to say something, then I was out the door in the cold once again. My eyes were drawn to the lake and the place where Pete had been found. Someone was standing there in a dark hoody, jeans and heavy winter boots.

They reached down to the ice and then put their hand in their pocket. My curiosity took over and I walked over to see who it was.

"Paul, how are you doing?" It was Paul the optometrist and Pete's close friend.

"Hey, Holly. I'm doing okay. I miss him a lot."

I couldn't help myself and blurted out, "did you find something? I saw you pick up something from the ice?"

Paul started. "Um yes, actually." He reached his hand back into his pocket and pulled something out. He extended his closed hand to me and then opened his fingers. It was a tiny gold star. Paul took a deep breath. "I think it's from Louella's glasses."

Opening my mouth to speak, the words failed to come out as we were interrupted by someone calling out to me. Paul immediately closed his hand and stuck it back in his pocket as we turned to greet the newcomer.

"Hello Meredith."

"Hello Holly, Paul. What are you two doing out here in the cold?" Once again she was dressed to the nines in a designer jacket, boots and gloves.

Paul spoke first. "Just paying my respects to Pete. He was my oldest and dearest friend."

Somehow Meredith managed to look contrite but her voice betrayed her. "Oh, I am so sorry for your loss Paul." She placed her hand on his shoulder for a moment. "I just came by to meet Travis. We're going to visit an escape room," she said excitedly.

I jumped on her words. "You should probably get going then. They are pretty sticky about their start times." The look on her face showed she hadn't really thought her comment through.

"You're probably right. Hey, why don't you double date with us? Travis has a friend I think you might like."

That was totally unexpected and it took me a moment to respond. "I don't know about that."

"Oh, you should," said Paul. "It might be fun." Was there a let's get Holly to date conspiracy going on? That was when I recalled that Vana knew Pete. That little sneak.

"Please say yes, Holly. It'll be great," implored Meredith. Unfortunately, my people pleasing self spoke before my brain engaged and I suddenly found myself agreeing to the date. "Great. Saturday night at Katie May's at 7 p.m. I just love that place, it's so casual and the food is so good." Without waiting for me to answer she started towards the candy shop, walking backwards so she could add, "don't stay out here too long, you might get sick from the cold." She spun around and hurried across the street and into the warm candy shop. I stopped watching after she went inside, not wanting to see her come back out with Travis.

I turned to look at Paul who was standing next to me watching Meredith. "Why did you encourage that?"

"The date? You're a nice person Holly, you really should enjoy your life more. Sometimes it's too short."

"Well, I can't argue with that. Why do you think the stone is from Louella's glasses?"

"She loved to have a tiny sparkle on all of her glasses. The side pieces of her old glasses had these on both sides. 'Just a little flare,' she said. I had to order them special and she was disappointed she couldn't get them for her new glasses." He turned to look at me with a serious look on his face.

"Holly, I know you solved Amos's murder and saved Jerry. Can you please look into this." His face was a mixture of sadness and anguish. "It can't be coincidence that Pete and Louella died within days of each other."

Instinctively I went to say 'I'm not a sleuth,' when I remembered that I actually did enjoy it. This was the third person who had found the deaths suspicious. Whoever the murderer was, they had been very sloppy. Instead I said, "of course I will. You're not the only one having suspicions. You should give that stone to Detective Smart. It could be a clue."

After promising me that he would and that he would be careful, we parted ways and I continued on with my raffle collections. Back at the office hours later, I surveyed the bounty and couldn't help but be pleased. This fall festival was going to be a huge success.

A ROUSING SUCCESS

By Friday evening the festival was in full swing. Maggs was supervising the ice skating in the backyard and it was a resounding success, especially as the rink in town still hadn't been opened. I would have to ask the Mayor what was taking so long. Patty and Meredith were upstairs with games for the younger kids, while the rest of the ladies were outside with booths for the messier games.

The bake sale was going strong, kids were bobbing for apples and showing off their pumpkin carving techniques. Lucy and Vana both had their grandkids here. I purchased some raffle tickets for Chloe and Penelope and made my way to the kitchen.

"How's everything going in here?" I asked Cindy. Women were neatly sorting cookies and cakes and portioning them out to platters.

"Just great," declared Cindy. "I think this is going to be the best festival ever."

I peered through the window into the backyard where kids were making rounds on the ice rink. "Maggs looks like she's having fun," I observed. Despite her age, Maggs was on the ice with the kids keeping order.

"She's like a kid in a candy store. Don't say anything but I think she used to be a professional skater," said Cindy.

"Really?" Patty looked dubious. Maggs was spinning in little circles as she watched the skaters go round the rink around her. Personally, I thought she might be getting a little dizzy.

"Oh, don't worry, she's just been doing a little nipping," said a masculine voice behind us.

"Charlie! I didn't know you were coming," cried Cindy. "It's so good to see you here. Sorry about your mom."

Charlie was Louella's son and looked remarkably like her. Tall and thin, with white hair which probably added to the resemblance. "How could I miss this? It was mum's favorite event. She always loved Halloween the most; the dressing up and especially the candy." He smiled remembering.

It was at that moment that I had a most brilliant idea. "Charlie, maybe we can get a plaque and dedicate the festival and the house to her. You know it's the first here in this place."

"Oh mum would love that," he said with tears in his eyes. His face grew serious. "She'd been coming up here a lot recently, I don't know why. I was starting to think she might want to buy this old place."

"I thought it was owned by the city? Isn't that why the festival was moved here?"

"Oh no," said Patty. "It's owned by the people who own the hotel by the lake. They donated it as a tax right off, I'm sure. Plus, it would take publicity away from Pete drowning in the lake just before the holiday season."

"Curious thing that," Charlie said quietly. He appeared to be lost in thought.

"What's that?" I asked.

"Pete and my mum, dying so closely together. Do you suppose there's a connection?"

"What kind of connection could there be?" I asked, thoroughly curious now, why people kept thinking something nefarious had happened.

"Somebody broke into Louella's house a few weeks ago. Nothing was taken, but it had been ransacked," he said.

"Why she never said a word about it," gasped Patty.

"Mildred's house was broken into recently also. Detective Smart said there's been a rash of break-ins recently," I added.

"You know Louella and Mildred used to work together in Castlemeyer. That's why Mildred moved here. Louella had told her what a delightful place it was. Of course it was more delightful 30 years ago," said Cindy. "I've got to take these trays out to the table now."

"Let me just help you with those," offered Charlie. They grabbed the trays of sweets and carried them off through the kitchen doors.

"I'm just going to go see if Maggs needs a break," said Patty. "She's getting a little wobbly out there." A cold draft blew through the door as she went outside. Maggs was indeed getting a bit wobbly on her skates. This left me alone in the kitchen wondering did Louella know about Betty? A sudden scream from the other room broke my thoughts.

BARNEY

Dashing through the door, I came to a screeching halt. Cindy and Charlie were backed up so tightly against the fireplace, they looked as if they were melting into it; terror etched across their faces. The trays of carefully prepared pastries were scattered across the table and floor. One donut had rolled all the way across the room. Of course I wasn't looking at any of this, oh no, my focus was on the large bear sitting in the middle of the room stuffing cream puffs in his mouth.

Barney had a puff in each paw and was taking turns taking a bite out of each one. I hissed at Cindy and Charlie, "you two, come this way slowly."

I was in a predicament, they were focussed solely on Barney and I didn't want to wave my hands and attract too much attention so I did the only thing I could under the circumstances. I threw a pumpkin muffin at them. I could have selected the blueberry but I really didn't want to damage their clothes.

The muffin caught Charlie square in the side of the face and I almost did a fist pump at my aim before recalling the bear. Charlie finally looked at me and I beckoned him to come my way. Charlie grabbed Cindy's hand and the two of them finally began edging themselves my way toward the kitchen.

Barney, glutton that he was, was thoroughly entranced with the pastries and didn't even glance our way. Once safely through the kitchen door, I blocked it with some chairs and everyone dashed outside, closing the door behind us.

Charlie and Cindy both heaved a sigh of relief. "That was so terrifying," she exclaimed. I thought I was going to die."

"Good choice to throw the pastries at him," I said to them both.

"That was more a reflex than a deliberate thing," said Charlie. "Bears are scary."

"But you have to admit, he did look quite cute with that dob of whip cream on his nose," I pointed out. Sorry to say Cindy and Charlie didn't feel the same as they both glared at me. "Why don't one of you go find the game wardens while I run around to the front and make sure no one goes in that way. The other one can stay here and clear everyone out."

In their eagerness to get away, they did a little tango before they got around each other and began shouting at the festival goers.

I ran around to the front, telling everyone to get away from the house as I did so. Seeing Travis, I yelled at him. "Travis, Barney's in the house. Where are the game wardens?"

"Barney?" he asked, puzzled.

"Oh, yes, the bear. There's a bear in the house."

"You named it?"

"Yes and it's in the house!"

"Well, okay, then. Let's go get it."

MURDER MOST FOUL

It took nearly an hour before the bear was tranquilized and packed off to be relocated. The community was extremely supportive and stuck around to finish the festival. Or because they wanted to see the bear up close. It was a toss up. Patty, Maggs, Cindy and I stood on the front porch and watched the warden's truck drive off.

"How did the bear get into the house in the first place?" asked Carol.

"I think someone left the window unlatched," said Cindy. "They must have, mustn't they?"

Carol scoffed. "Who would do such a thing?"

"We were trying to be so careful," said Patty.

"I personally checked all the windows myself," declared Maggs. "Was someone in here while we were gone?"

"Well now that it's gone, let's check all the windows and make sure it can't get back in. We're just lucky no one got hurt," I said.

We all scurried off in different directions. A short time later a scream rang out. We all rushed to the sound, cautiously in case it was another bear. Honestly, I couldn't tell one bear from another and I wasn't sure it was the same one that had come back.

Dashing into a downstairs room that turned out to be a study, we found Carol standing over a body holding a knife which she dropped at our approach.

"Oh, my God is that Paul?" I asked shocked. I had just spoken to him recently.

"I didn't do it. I didn't do it." repeated Carol over and over.

145

Putting my arms around her shoulders, I turned her and led her out of the room. "Of course you didn't honey. Everybody out. Maggs, shut the door and don't let anyone in. Patty, go find an officer."

"Why is it always me?" whined Maggs. I rolled my eyes and growled at her and she wisely shut up. I led Carol to a chair and sat her down.

"Now Carol, tell me what happened."

Carol took a couple deep breaths. I went into the room to check the windows and he was just there, lying on the floor, dead!" she said in a shrill voice, starting to hyperventilate.

"Look at me Carol. Breathe slowly." We stared at each other as she tried to follow my directions with shaky breaths. "One, two, three. Let it out, one, two, three." Her breathing became steady again as she calmed down. Asking her more questions would be pointless at this point as it would just excite her again. By this time Patty was back with Travis and she pointed to the door.

"He's in there." Her arm fell to her side as if it was too heavy for her to hold up.

"I was watching the door. No one went inside," confirmed Maggs.

"Thank you, You can leave now." He stepped into the room and I watched as he knelt by Paul's side and took his pulse. He looked up at me and shook his head slightly. So Paul was definitely gone.

As usual, Meredith followed the officers as they met up with Travis, spotting the bloody knife on the floor, she exclaimed, "Bonnie has a set just like that." I glanced again at the knife. It was a standard kitchen knife and unremarkable except for its handle which was a brilliant orange. How many people in Appleby used a set of orange kitchen knives? I may not like Bonnie but this didn't feel right. Bonnie may be a lot of things but she's also crafty. After all, she'd spent the last five years undermining my business without me catching on. She was also slightly psychotic, relishing the moment I finally uncovered the truth, like she had been waiting for just that moment her whole life.

Murdering someone in a public place and leaving the weapon behind didn't fit her.

SPEAK OF THE DEVIL

The officers finally ushered us all out and we waited in the back yard where the games were still going on. Not ten minutes later, a sudden screeching reached my ears. "Holly, is this how you secure festivals? A bear and a murder in one evening?"

I cringed at her words. So far, no one else knew about the murder. The sounds of merriment died away and everyone turned to look at Bonnie standing by the corner of the house.

"Is it another bear?"

"Who died?"

Questions began to pepper the air as parents grabbed their children close. I stepped forward to wrest control from her before there was more damage. "Folks it's not another bear. Everyone's safe. I'm sorry to say that there has been an unfortunate incident and the police are going to want to talk to you. If you would please all wait here." I smiled at them all. "I'm sure it would be all right if the kids continued playing. It might be better if they are distracted."

Bonnie opened her mouth to speak again and Maggs stepped in front of her. "I don't think that this is the best time do you?" She glared down at Bonnie from her nearly six foot height. Bonnie squinted her eyes at her furiously but stood down. Maggs gave her a beautiful smile. "Besides, I think the police probably want to talk to you, considering you're the Mayor's liaison."

Bonnie grunted, made an ugly face at Maggs and then stomped inside.

"Thank you Maggs, I really appreciate that," I said quietly to her as we watched the police stop Bonnie inside. "I notice you didn't warn her."

"Sometimes karma gives us a gift and we should just sit back and enjoy it, don't you think?" Then she winked at me.

"You sneaky..." I began before being rudely interrupted again.

"The police just arrested Bonnie for Paul's murder!" yelled Meredith as she dashed out the kitchen door. Once again all the voices stopped as everyone turned to look at her.

"Wow. Meredith. Do you think maybe the police wanted to tell everyone themselves? A lot of people here were friends with him."

Meredith's face reddened with embarrassment. She licked her lips and breathed in deeply. "I'm so sorry, I wasn't thinking. I'm sorry," she called louder to everyone within hearing distance.

"What were you doing in there anyway? We were all supposed to leave," demanded Patty.

"Were you snooping?" asked Gloria hopefully.

"If you must know," she said in a low voice. "I had to use the restroom."

"Sure you did," said Maggs. By this time people were gathering around Meredith and peppering her with questions. Maggs grabbed my arm and pulled me out of the way as Meredith put on, what I now call, her hysterical act. Oh, she was good. People began to hug her and offer her commiserations. She didn't say it, but she thoroughly implied that she was the one who found the body.

"Grandma, grandma, did someone really die?" cried out Chloe. Penelope was doing her best to calm her down but even at four, Chloe could tell when something bad happened.

I knelt down and gave her a hug. "Everything is going to be okay," I said comfortingly. How dare Meredith and Bonnie deliberately scare all these children. I looked around at the commotion going on. I mentally crossed my fingers that karma would get both of them.

Travis stepped into the backyard, followed by several officers who fanned out amongst the crowd. "If I could get everyone's attention," he said in a loud voice. "We've had an unfortunate incident here tonight and someone has died. The officers here are going to get your statements and then you will be free to leave."

"I thought you arrested Bonnie," yelled a voice. I could have sworn that Travis looked at Meredith as he grimaced.

"We are just asking her questions. No one has been arrested. Please just cooperate with the officers and we'll get through this as quickly as we can."

AFTERMATH

Four hours later, I sat exhausted on my couch with a cup of hot chocolate. Everyone had been questioned and left. The ladies and I weren't going to be allowed to clean anything up until after the investigation was done but I did get permission for us to remove all the food from the premises and donate it to the local food bank. Yes, even in the small town of Appleby, we had people who could use it and the excess would go to Morecroft which had more of a problem.

Travis promised he would let us know as soon as the investigation was done although I wasn't looking forward to returning to this house again.

I swirled my cup and watched the marshmallows melt. I needed to relax so I could sleep. In the morning I was going to call the book club for an emergency meeting.

Paul's murder was proof that Pete and Louella were also murdered. It was too much of a coincidence that they all knew each other. My mind swirled in circles. What was the connection? Did the break-ins have anything to do with them? Mildred and Louella had both lived in Castlemeyer. And Meredith. Did her previous case have anything to do with this? What reason would Bonnie have to kill Paul? He was just the local optometrist. Was that it? Louella had ordered new glasses from him. She lost hers in someone's car or did she? The message had cut off, maybe she had found them and then dropped them in the bushes. At this rate, I was never getting to sleep. With a sigh, I walked around the house making sure all the doors and windows were locked. When I got back to the front door, there was an envelope laying on the floor. If someone had come by recently, the dogs hadn't barked. Maybe it was there the whole time and I just hadn't noticed it. I did come in through the garage, so maybe. I turned it over in my hands. My name was printed in block letters on the front.

Inside it contained a single sheet of paper.

Your husband isn't who you think he is, was scrawled across the page.

What the heck did that mean and why would someone say that now? He's been dead for ten years. I looked at Ginger and she looked at me. "Ginger, did someone come by the house? You would have let me know, right?" Ginger whined and laid her head on her paws. "C'mon, let's go to bed. If someone breaks in, you can bite them okay?" She wagged her tail furiously then jumped off the couch and bounded down the hall to the bedroom. I followed behind, yawning. Maybe I could finally fall asleep.

APPREHENSION

It's Saturday and I am not looking forward to tonight. I agreed to a double date with Travis and Meredith and his friend. With last night's situation, I crossed my fingers that he would call to cancel. I certainly wasn't going to be the one to do it. I called the murder club ladies together for a meeting this morning and attempted to tidy the house before they arrived.

"Ladies, thank you all for coming over on such short notice." Maggs, Cindy, Mildred, Gloria and I all gathered around the kitchen table with a pad of sticky notes and a pen. Cindy had scrounged up an old bulletin board from somewhere and Mildred had brought sticky buns and orange juice. I supplied the coffee. I filled them in on my thoughts from the previous evening and we set about to make our first 'murder board.'

"We've really got to solve this before someone else gets killed," declared Gloria. "I love this little town but lately," she let the comment hang and shook her head sadly.

"I vote for Meredith," said Cindy, half raising her hand before letting it fall sheepishly.

"That's not how this works," said Mildred. "You don't vote. We have to decipher the clues."

Taking back control I said, "Let's go over what we know." I grabbed a bite of a sticky bun and set it back on the plate. "First we have Pete. If he was murdered, what clues do we have?" I reached for the pencil to write his name but my fingers were sticky, so I licked them off, with my sticky tongue. Shaking her head at me, Gloria wrote Pete's name on a sticky note and placed it on the board while I ran my hand under the

155

faucet. Drying my hands on a towel, I began again. Mildred grabbed my plate and pulled it out of my reach.

"Pete," she said.

"Yes, Pete. Okay, so we know that he was frozen in the ice which means that he got placed there sometime overnight because the lake wasn't frozen that afternoon. Mistake one for our murderer. Alex, his son, said he was wearing the wrong clothes and Betty said he hated fishing."

Cindy raised her hand again. "Yes, Cindy," I sighed. If you can't beat 'em, join 'em right?

"Perhaps we oughtn't to use her name."

"How about Gertrude," said Mildred. "I've always loved the name Gertrude."

"Fine. Gertrude said he hated fishing. So who put him out there? Was he drugged? How did the murderer incapacitate him? We need to find out."

"Oh, oh, I have a friend in the police department. I'll ask her," said Cindy.

"Is it Joanna?" questioned Maggs.

"It might be," said Cindy defensively.

"I'll ask Joanna," I said. Cindy crossed her arms and gave Maggs a sulky look. "I sold her mom a house," I added in explanation. "Now onto the next victim." I wrote Louella's name and placed it on the board. "Mildred received a voice message from Louella and we could hear her looking for her glasses in someone's car." Mildred played the message for everyone. "Unfortunately, there's not a time so we don't know if it was from that morning."

"Why don't you just look at your phone records?" asked Maggs.

"You can do that?" marveled Mildred. Maggs gave her a mom look.

"I'll check into that."

I continued on. "Pete was giving Louella rides into town because she can't see without her glasses and they live across the street from each other."

"Oh, he was such a nice man," gushed Cindy. After glares from the others she clarified, "Outside of the fall festival I mean. You are a much better chairperson." She smiled at me.

"Maybe, the killer killed Pete at his house and thought Louella saw him or her. Maybe they didn't know she couldn't see that far," suggested Maggs. I paused to think. That would definitely link the two together and was a good motive.

"Excellent thought Maggs. But why would they kill Paul?" I asked. "His death doesn't make any sense. Obviously, he knew that Louella's glasses were broken because he ordered the new ones. If we can find out why he was killed I believe we will have our murderer. What about the break-ins? Could they be connected?"

"Oh, I don't think so," said Mildred. "It was just vacant houses."

"Yours wasn't," I pointed out.

"Maybe they are escalating? I heard criminals do that sometimes," she said.

"Hmm, maybe," I said, but there was a tickling in my brain. Mildred was hiding something. "I think I'll drop by the station and see if Joanna knows when they might release the crime scene. It's the weekend, maybe you ladies can get some snooping in."

I stopped by the bakery on my way into town and got a big box of donuts for the station. It might be cliche but everyone loves donuts. I carried the big box in and set it on Joanna's desk. I knew she was working because she'd been kind of bummed about having to leave the fall festival early to get to work in the morning.

"Hello Joanna," I said brightly, looking around the eerily quiet room. "I brought you all some donuts. Is everyone off today?"

"Hi Holly. No, most of them are up at the Blume House investigating." I took the lid off the pink box and she reached in for a cake donut with sprinkles. "Did you hear Bonnie got arrested for Paul's murder?"

I tried not to look too happy about that. "I thought they were just questioning her?"

"Oh, no. They went to her house last night and the same exact knife was missing from her set," she added in a low voice. "You should have seen her protesting. She kept repeating, 'I'll have the Mayor after you for this.'" Joanna lowered her voice to imitate Bonnie's and she was pretty good.

I blinked a few times. "Wow." As much as I wanted it to be true, there was no way it could be. She had no reason to kill Pete or Louella. "Joanna, just between you and me, was there anything suspicious about Pete or Louella's deaths?"

Joanna looked around quickly. "Travis thinks Pete was dead before he was put in the lake but the coroner won't commit to that. He's suspicious that Louella fell too." Footsteps sounded in the hallway.

"Thanks Joanna," I whispered back. In a louder voice I said, "Do you know when they might release the crime scene? We really need to return all the rental items and lock up the house before it snows."

"Don't answer that," snapped Detective Moran. "It'll be released when the investigation is over and not a moment sooner."

"Oh, hello Detective, "I didn't know you were back in town."

"Yes, I am and I'll be taking over the investigation from here on out and I don't need any snoopy two-bit wanna-be detective getting in my way."

I wanted to snap back at him, but the professional part of me thankfully took over. "Nobody is snooping into anything, Detective Moran. As the chairman of the festival I need to be fiscally responsible with the town's money and would like to get the rental items returned as quickly as possible." I ended with a smile I didn't feel.

"I heard you were doing that. Don't know why they didn't give that position to Miss Belmar, she's much better suited for it." He sneered as he said it. A lightbulb clicked in my head and his animosity suddenly made sense. Just how deep did Bonnie's treachery go? Bonnie blamed me for getting, what she called, the ugly girl's face. In the car accident that killed my husband, she went through the windshield and the glass had ruined her face. Due to her parents' money and influence, she became a recipient for a face transplant. A comment spoken in my grief to the dead woman's husband, Detective Travis, and he rescinded the donation of his wife's face. Now she blamed me and had been trying to ruin my life ever since. "Thank you for the information, detective. I'll be waiting for your call." I walked away, smiling to myself.

WITH NO PHONE CALL to save me, I resigned myself to the fact that I was going on a date. On the positive side, maybe I could pick up some useful information about the investigations and last night's murder. I dressed in jeans and a nice shirt and fed Ginger. I gave her an extra crunchy bone. No reason she should feel put out and then drove the twenty minutes into town. Katie May's was pretty busy on a Saturday night and the noise hit my ears as I opened the door. Katie caught my eye as I entered and twitched her head in the direction of the back of the cafe. Travis and Meredith were already sitting at a table for four along with a handsome blonde guy.

He and Travis stood up as I approached and Travis introduced us. "This is Scott Williams from the police department in Morecroft. He and I have been working together for several years now. I shook his hand and he waited until I was seated to sit as well.

"Hello Scott, nice to meet you. Travis has told me nothing about you." Everyone laughed.

"I have to admit that I'm the one that bugged him to meet you. You have quite the reputation in town."

"I hope it's a good one," I replied.

"Of course it is," said Travis and Scott at nearly the same time.

"Everyone in town loves you Holly," said Meredith. "Sorry for the short notice but everyone was free today and that doesn't always happen. Scott just got back from a big investigation and of course Travis is here helping."

"Speaking of investigations, how is Paul's murder going? I heard you arrested Bonnie?"

The waitress chose that moment to come and ask us for our orders and I was afraid I wasn't going to get an answer but after she left, Travis answered my question.

"They brought her in for questioning. I've been off all day so I don't know what happened. Chief Moran is back and he seems to have a grudge against me. She will probably get out on bail soon, if they even charge her."

"Don't worry, the department is still short so he'll have to let you continue investigating," said Scott sympathetically.

"Any update on the break-ins? Mildred said the guy who tried to rob her isn't speaking," I asked.

Travis looked at Scott and then shook his head. "Nope. We haven't gotten anywhere with that. The guy got transferred over to Morecroft to be processed. Apparently, he committed some thefts there also."

Meredith looked at him curiously. "He's not going to be prosecuted here?"

Scott answered her question. "No. They will just add it to his charges and sentence him in Morecroft. It happens all the time with these small towns."

The waitress brought our food and we spent the next several minutes enjoying our meals. Scott told us about some of his crazier arrests while we ate. He seemed to be a very funny guy but my questions kept running through my mind. Meredith was actually a very intelligent, interesting person who had a lot of insights into people's characters. At the end of the evening, I had to admit, I had actually enjoyed myself.

ESTATE SALE

L ouise already had the estate sale signs up directing people to Betty's house as I made my way there Saturday morning. We had two days to sell all her belongings and then the rest would be donated to charity. I already had the house listed and had flyers ready to hand out. I parked in the driveway next to Louise's car.

I put the flyers in the plastic box fastened to the for sale sign in the front yard and made my way into the house. It was going to be weird selling Betty's belongings when I knew she was still alive. Well that and lying to everyone.

"Hi Louise, looks like you've done a great job here." Everything was all laid out neatly with price tags.

"Thanks Holly, I really do enjoy my job," she replied. "Oh and here." She reached to a table behind her and grabbed a small cardboard box. "I don't usually do this. It's weird, you know, that people buy old photos of people they don't even know, but they do. Anyway, I saved these for you."

She handed me the box and I lifted the lid. Inside were the photos from Betty's dresser drawer. "I could see how much Betty meant to you. Maybe you could give me a token amount for them? Say $5?"

"I'll do you one better and give you $100 since the proceeds are for the kids," I replied. I hadn't even thought to ask for them. The next few hours were busy as we sold items and made change. A few potential buyers made their way through the home. It wasn't until Sunday that Jacob showed up wearing a neon green tracksuit.

"Are you interested in buying the house?" I asked him.

"Why would I want to buy this piece of junk?" he snarled back. He never has been the most pleasant.

"Well, it's right next door to Carol's house. I thought maybe you would be interested."

A disgusted look crossed his face and he made as if to speak but thought better of it. "I just really like Carol's old house. It's perfect for me. So, just let me know if they ever want to sell." He poked his head through a few doors and then left.

"He's a strange one," remarked Louise.

"Yeah, strange," I answered. Why did Jacob care so much about Carol's house? There wasn't anything special about it, other than all the dead animal bones in the backyard, which was disclosed to the buyers. Thankfully, they were animal lovers too. I dismissed him from my mind and helped Louise to clean and lock up.

All in all it was a great weekend, barring the bear and the death at the festival. We ended up making a great deal of money from both events and most of Betty's things had been sold. Louise would make arrangements to donate the rest to charity and give me a final accounting of the funds.

It was a lovely thing that Betty had done, donating the money from her house and possession to the elementary school library. They would really put the money to good use. It was horrible that she had to fake her own death just to get away from her sister.

DEVELOPMENTS

I met Joanna Monday morning at Katie May's where I requested a back booth. Joanna wasn't your typical reporter. She was a beautiful Hispanic woman who looked like she was still in school.

"You must have begun reporting as a toddler," I said to her.

She laughed. "Yes, when I was five." She waited while Katie brought us coffee then she laid a fat folder on the table and kept her hand pressed on it. "I don't even know where to start with this. It's mostly suppositions on my part and I don't really have any proof."

I delayed answering by pouring sugar and creamer into my coffee and giving it a long stir. Setting the spoon carefully on the saucer, I let out the breath I had been holding and said, "Just tell me straight."

"Okay. You're right. Meredith Maroney was the fourth person in the car. It took me ages to find her. Whoever they paid to hide the facts behind this accident was really good. Of course, that only made me more curious. What I've finally put together over the years is this."

I listened silently while she laid out all of her facts and suppositions. "The four women had grown up together and had made a pact to never have children. It was Lana's dictate really. She was beautiful and wanted to be admired by her friends forever. Apparently, she was a little psychotic.

"They were going to meet Meredith's boyfriend at the lookout. Lana Wentworth was driving, her sister Hope in the seat behind her. Laura Wexler was in the front seat and Meredith was in the back next to Hope. Laura told them all that she was pregnant which infuriated Lana so she drove her car into the oncoming car on Laura's side. The car spun out and went over the side.

"Meredith had a nervous breakdown and spent the next five years in and out of mental institutions. Laura died and Lana's family paid for her to have a face transplant. I don't know what happened but she didn't get Laura's face, I guess the husband changed his mind. It took nearly five years for Lana to get over the fact she was no longer beautiful. She kept hoping the next surgery would fix her."

I pressed my hand against my chest. I couldn't breathe. "Wait, that's wrong. Bonnie, Lana, was drunk."

Joanna shook her head sadly. "No. The parents felt it was better to have her drunk than a psychopath."

"I don't understand. You said Meredith's boyfriend died, but it was my husband that died." Am I suffocating? I feel like I'm suffocating. I closed my eyes. "Evan. Evan was my husband."

I felt her grab my hand. "Holly, look at me." I opened my eyes to see her holding a glass of water in front of me. "Take a drink."

I felt the cold water travel all the way down to my belly where it sat uncomfortably. "I don't understand. How do you know all this?"

Joanna bit her lip before answering, inadvertently making herself look even younger. Then speaking in a very low voice she continued. "Lana's parents died in a car accident. Except, they didn't. I tracked them down. Remember I said Lana was a psycho? They became afraid of her and so they faked their deaths. Lana blamed them for her wrong choices. They told me all this, that's why I can't prove it. They think she sabotaged their car so they made the best of it. You called her Bonnie?"

I nodded my head. "Yes. She changed her name to Bonnie Belmar. I just found out last month and her sister confirmed it."

"Can I talk to her sister?"

I looked her in the eyes and then shook my head slowly. "She died of cancer last month."

Joanna stared at me for a moment and then nodded to herself. "Okay."

"Meredith Maroney was having an affair with my husband?" I asked, hoping desperately to confirm that that was just a guess.

"I told you I was sorry about what I had to tell you."

"Are you sure? I had no idea."

"Most women don't. There's an outlook on the road and that's where they were heading. He had just picked up his cat from getting fixed at the vet and he was going to meet Meredith there. I'm sorry."

"That bastard killed my cat. I loved that cat." I sobbed. "Is that why she's in town? To rub it in my face? Is this another plan of Bonnie's to get revenge on me?"

Joanna looked concerned. "Why would she want revenge on you?"

"I guess you don't know everything. Apparently, I'm the one that prevented her from getting Laura's face." I let out a bitter laugh. "I guess I don't feel so bad about that anymore. Thank you Joanna for coming out here and telling me the truth. Don't worry, your secrets are safe with me."

She nodded her head. "I'm glad to finally meet you. And to let you know the truth. It's been eating me up all these years, thinking you were grieving over that two-timing...Anyway, I should get out of here. I don't need Lana or Meredith spotting me."

Lucy and Vana were sitting with me after lunch. I told them all about what I found out about how Evan was supposedly cheating on me and I used that word because I couldn't believe it.

"Tell me about him," said Lucy. "You never really talk about him.

I thought back over the years to our marriage. "What can I say? He was the sweetest, most thoughtful man I've ever met. We had a beautiful daughter and now we have a granddaughter that he never got to see." The terrible emptiness and sadness I felt when she was born, that he wasn't there, came over me in a flood. "Penelope had missed him terribly after the accident and Chloe never had a chance to meet her charming, sweet, thoughtful grandfather. She would have loved him."

"He sounds like he was a wonderful man," said Lucy. "I don't think you really believe that he cheated on you."

I don't know where the words came from but they just spouted out of my mouth. "I don't. He didn't. There's no way. I will never believe it." After telling Lucy and Vanna about Evan I felt something stirring deep down inside of me and when it finally came to the surface I recognized it for what it was Ethan had loved me and I knew that from the bottom of my toes to the top of my head he had been my soulmate and I was his and I knew that he would never never have cheated on me. He was not that kind of person. When I was with Evan, there was never a doubt in my mind about his honesty and integrity and I wasn't going to believe it now either. "I don't know how she did it, but you can be assured that this is Bonnie's doing."

Vana took my hand. "This happened before Bonnie knew what you did. No, no hear me out. This happened just after the accident."

"What are you saying?" I demanded.

"Did Bonnie have an issue with Meredith? She told her that her boyfriend was killed. Isn't that why she ended up in the asylum? And we never found out her name until Joanna told you. It was never in the papers. Maybe that was deliberate. Why would she hide Meredith's name when everyone else's name was listed?"

She had something there. Something I had never thought about. She deliberately steered into that car because Laura said she was pregnant. Why would she torture Meredith? What else happened that day?

I laid in bed staring at the ceiling while Ginger snored quietly next to me. Thoughts plagued me. Evan wouldn't cheat on me, so who was Meredith's boyfriend? Why had he never contacted her? I sat up suddenly in bed. Her name wasn't in the papers! Is that why? What happened that day that made Bonnie want to destroy Laura and Meredith's lives? My brain tickled as if there was something I needed to remember but the more I thought about it, the less it came to me.

I went to my kitchen and grabbed some paper and a pen and started writing the clues down.

★ Evan and our cat died coming back from the vet.

★ Laura just announced she was pregnant.

★ Meredith was going to meet her boyfriend. What was his name?

★ Neither Meredith's name or picture was in the papers. Why were the others listed and not her?

★ They were going to meet Meredith's boyfriend who also had a cat at the turnout.

EXCEPT THEY WEREN'T. That was what was bothering me. They would have slowed down to make the turn onto the lookout. I had deliberately avoided that section of highway but I was positive I was right. If that was the case, Bonnie wouldn't have had enough speed for the car to kill Laura.

I needed to bring this information to the book club. I was too close to the situation. Maybe Bonnie did kill Pete, Louella and Paul. I tried to believe that but the little angel on my shoulder kept asking me why, why, why? Every crime needs a motive, even a crime of passion.

If Evan hadn't cheated on me (which he didn't) then maybe there was another answer. Could it possibly be a coincidence that two men with cats were going to be on the same road at the same time? What was it she had said? My cat was already fixed, she was coming home from getting vaccinated at the vet. Did they do autopsies on cats? Would there be any evidence of the cat in the police reports?

Meredith had gone to the mental hospital, her name was never mentioned in the paper so if she had just disappeared maybe her boyfriend was still out there. Bonnie had manipulated that part of the conversation too to keep Meredith under her control. What I had to do was find Meredith's boyfriend and to do that first I needed to speak to Meredith.

TRAVIS CALLED ON TUESDAY morning to let us know that we could clear out the house, so I notified all the ladies and we met up at the Blume House where I had a burning question to ask the ladies.

"I really need to know," I began. "Why is this house considered haunted?"

The ladies all glanced at each other and then Patty began, "People have said they have seen lights on at night when no one was here."

"And kids have snuck up here and said things moved around when no one was looking."

I couldn't resist, "Who's this no one and why do they keep coming up here?" The ladies all looked at me blankly. "Okay, it was a bad joke. I admit it. What kind of things moved?"

"Well, my son said there was a chair in a room upstairs and it moved downstairs all by itself," said Cindy.

"Is that it? That's not very spooky," I said. "No apparitions?" I was beginning to think it was just Betty and her friend.

"Rumor is a worker died during construction of the home," added Cindy, "but I guess that's typical of haunted houses."

Gloria jumped in excitedly, "Maybe it's cursed. Louella died and now poor Paul." She dropped her head sadly.

The talk of ghosts made me shiver as I opened the front door which opened soundlessly as I pushed on it. "Look, not even a creak. Let's get this done and get home."

The ladies all excitedly pushed through the door and stopped in the doorway. "Well would you look at that?" Marveled Mildred.

I squeezed through and found that all the party items had been stacked neatly inside the front room. "Huh." I said, puzzled. "Maybe the police did it? Or maybe, the Mayor had someone come by. You know he had it cleaned before we set up." The ladies looked a bit crestfallen as I gave a non ghostly explanation. "Why don't you all go through the house and make sure everything is locked up and that the cleaners didn't miss anything."

I walked through the house, surveying each room. I hesitated at the door to the room Paul died in. With a determined effort, I opened it and walked inside. I'm a real estate agent after all and it's my responsibility to make sure that everything is ship shape. There was no evidence that anyone had ever died in here. I double checked the window but it was locked.

I stood still for a moment, listening. Nope, no creepy feeling, no weird noises. I couldn't even hear the other ladies walking around upstairs. Wouldn't there be a creepy feeling if it was haunted? I returned to the front hall to wait for the rest of the ladies.

"Everything upstairs is copacetic," announced Meredith in a cheery voice. "Where's Carol today? She's supposed to be here helping. "She left me high and dry during the festival too."

"She did what?" I asked.

"She left me during the event. I had to handle two rooms by myself. Said she was going to the restroom."

"You can't fault someone for using the restroom, Meredith. There were supposed to be volunteers to help when someone needed a break."

Meredith huffed, "I needed to use the restroom too and she took forever."

"I'm sorry that happened to you but you did get to use the restroom when she came back."

"That's just it, she didn't come back and now she's not here today," I just hate flaky people," she muttered.

One by one, the other ladies filed back into the room and gave the same report, everything was locked up and put away.

"That's great," I said. "Let's haul all this stuff out to our cars. The rental people should be here any minute to pick up the tables and chairs. Has anyone heard from Carol?"

"Oh, yes," said Mildred. "Her son got sick, she's been taking care of him all week. I'm sorry, I thought you knew."

I gave Meredith the look that mom's save for belligerent children. "Thank you Mildred. I'll check in on her when I get back and see if she needs anything. She was supposed to help me deliver the raffle items, can anyone else help me with that?"

Cindy raised her hand, "I can. Oh, but we haven't pulled the names yet, we don't know who won."

"That's okay, dear," replied Mildred. "Just bring them all to my shop and we can pick the names there and the winners can come by and pick them up. That way you won't have to drive all over town delivering them."

"Thank you Mildred, that's very nice of you," I said. "Okay ladies, all the raffle items can go in mine and Cindy's cars and anyone who wants to help draw names, meet us there and I'll buy you all an ice cream sundae." The little devil started to grumble about spending money on people but the angel of kindness bopped him on the head and shut him up. Forty-five minutes later and the rental people were gone and our cars were all loaded. I locked the front door and drove away without once looking back. This was one house I would be glad not to return to.

On the way to the candy shop I stopped by City Hall to drop off the house key. "Hello Alda," I addressed the mayor's secretary who looked as chic as ever. "I'm just returning the Blume house key." She took the key from my hand and tucked it into an envelope which she then wrote the name on. "Oh, and be sure to tell the mayor thanks for cleaning the house before and after the event. I don't know who the cleaning crew was, but they did a tremendous job. Do you suppose I could get their name?"

Alda looked at me puzzled. "Cleaning crew? The mayor didn't have the house cleaned before or after the event."

"Are you sure? It was spotless when we first went there. Cindy said the mayor had a full crew come in and clean."

"I see why you're confused," she relaxed and smiled. "It had been discussed at a council meeting but it was never approved. Honestly, it's a vacant house, how dirty could it get? A little sweeping and maybe mopping the floor. That's why they decided not to hire someone."

Maybe she was right and it never had been very dirty. The windows were all sealed and it was surrounded by trees, not a lot of dirt in the first place. I smiled brightly, "thank you, Alda. In case anyone asks, we'll be doing the raffle drawings today at Mildred's and then notifying the winners, not that that is probably anyone's real concern right now after what happened. But just in case."

Alda nodded as she dropped the envelope into her desk drawer. In a lower voice she said, "Just between you and me, the mayor feels you did a wonderful job considering. You don't think Bonnie really killed someone do you?" Conflicting emotions crossed my mind. What should I say? I can't say that I don't like her and she deserves it. Finally, I committed to, "I can't see that she really has any motive to do so and there usually is a strong motive. Have you heard anything?"

Alda shook her head. "The mayor is pretty upset, three upstanding citizens killed and on top of the break ins, it's not good."

"So he does think they were murdered?"

"More so after Paul's death. The break-ins are weird too."

"How so?"

"Nothing has been taken. And then Mildred's home while she was there. Pete and Louella's homes too. It's such an outrage that someone would do that while their loved ones are at their funeral."

I couldn't hide my shock. "Someone broke into Pete and Louella's homes?"

Alda nodded her head. "You should talk to Detective Smart. He's been investigating the crimes." She suddenly put her hand over her mouth. "Oh, I'm sorry, it's probably awkward for you with that woman hanging all over him all the time."

"It's fine. He's entitled to see who he wants. Besides, it's not like we're dating or anything." I shrugged as I said it but I didn't feel it. "So nothing was ever stolen. What do you think they were after?"

"Detective Moran thinks it's just kids causing trouble." Alda bit her lip and looked around before speaking quietly. "Did you know that Pete and Louella used to date in high school? Then later they both worked at the same bank together. There was a huge scandal and they moved here."

"A scandal?"

"Mm, hmm. Somebody robbed the bank. The money was stolen and never recovered. Do you think that's why someone broke into the houses?"

"But they broke into Mildred's house too. That doesn't make any sense. And what about all the cabins?"

"I suppose not. Maybe the mayor's right and it's just kids up to no good."

I smiled at her comfortingly, because it's my job and I could tell she was scared. It's a common technique to blame someone or try to find the reason when a crime occurs. It helps people to feel safe and that they aren't at risk. "I'm sure they will catch them soon. In the meantime, you could install some cameras and motion sensor lights. I hear they work well at scaring off criminals."

I said my goodbyes and walked to my car but my mind was occupied by the thought of something the robber had asked Mildred. Was she in danger?

I ran into Carol at the market when I stopped by to pick up a quick snack. Okay, it was powdered donuts, don't judge. "Hello Carol, how's your son doing?"

"Oh, I'm so sorry Holly. I thought Meredith had told you I was going to be out of town. But, yes, my son is doing great now. The doctors say it was just a really bad case of the flu and he's on the mend."

"Well there's nothing like having your mom there to take care of you when you're ill." Unless it's my mom and then you're better off taking care of yourself. You said you told Meredith to tell me?"

"Oh yes, but she's so flaky. Do you know she left me alone with all those kids for over 30 minutes. Said she was running to the bathroom. Who takes 30 minutes in the bathroom?"

"I am so sorry about that Carol. Next time, we'll have a roving assistant who can check in on everyone regularly."

"Oh? Are you volunteering again next year?"

"Oh. Well, I hadn't really thought about it. I was really just going to put it in the suggestions."

"But that's not what you said." She looked at me hopefully.

I took a deep breath. "Maybe," I said slowly. "I'll think about it."

"You do that because this was the most fun I've ever had at the festival. You really brought a happy spirit to the event," she gushed.

CONFRONTATION

I found Meredith sitting alone on the bench near where Pete died, looking out at the lake.

"Meredith. Would you mind if I sat with you?"

She didn't even glance up at me, she just snugged her coat a bit tighter to block out the cold wind. "Whatever."

"Are you okay?" I asked as I sat next to her. I pulled the donuts out and offered her one.

"Thanks. I think I might go back to Castlemeyer," she said, pinching a donut with her fingers. "Things aren't working out for me here." For some reason that made me really happy.

"I'm sorry to hear that." I stared out at the lake wondering how to begin. The edges of the lake were frozen and slush piled up every time the wind blew a wave over it. Another month and it would be entirely frozen over. I shivered and decided to just go for it.

"I'm confused. Why does Gloria call you a sleuth? By your own admission, you just made a phone call."

"That's my fault. You know how Gloria tends to blow things up. I just went along with it. Sometimes I think she needs a hero." Thinking back I could see the truth in it.

Is that why you were there? Looking for the money? Another thought struck me. "Are you behind the break-ins here?"

Meredith turned at this question and looked at me. "Are you crazy? I don't know who those people are. Why would you ask me that?"

"Sorry, sometimes my brain leaps to conclusions. You were looking for the money though, right?"

"Yes," she confessed. "I have a lot of bills. The money would have really helped me and no one has ever found it."

I took a wild guess. "Medical bills?"

Her eyes widened. "How did you know?"

"Joanna told me. It's because of Bonnie, from the accident right?"

She scooted back to the end of the bench and narrowed her eyes at me suspiciously. I sighed. "I know Bonnie is Lana Wentworth and that she caused the accident that put you in the hospital. I also know that she's an evil vindictive person." I could see Meredith begin to relax a little bit. "I really just need to know what your boyfriend's name was." I looked at her hopefully.

"It was Colin Gray." She suddenly burst into tears. "I loved him so much. He just asked me to marry him. He had the ring tied around Purry's neck. It was so perfect. Then Lana, Hope and Laura picked me up and I never saw him again."

I sat there stunned. She had left her boyfriend. "Bonnie lied."

"What?" she sniffled.

"Bonnie lied to you. It wasn't your boyfriend that died. It was my husband, who also had a cat. He was coming back from the vet with him. I've got to go. Don't trust Bonnie and don't let her know I talked to you."

I hurried off and called the ladies from the book club for an emergency meeting. "I have some new information," I said as we all gathered in my living room. I filled them all in on the details I had learned from Meredith and Joanna. "So you see, I'm afraid it might very well have been Bonnie."

The ladies looked doubtful.

"What?"

Cindy spoke up first. "You were pretty convinced it was Meredith."

"Correction, I may have been wishing it was Meredith."

"Because she's stealing your beau," piped in Maggs.

"He is not my beau," I said defensively, "we are just..."

"We know," cut in Gloria. "But you're just lying to yourself. I've seen how you look at him."

Mildred cleared her throat, catching our attention. "There's a problem with your theories. Louella only began dating Pete after he moved to Appleby. Before that he was dating me. I was the teller at the bank when it got robbed. We always felt it was an inside job. So if your theory is that the thieves were targeting Pete and Louella for the jewels, then how does Paul fit into it?"

"So the thieves were looking for you!" I exclaimed.

Mildred looked apologetic. "Yes. I'm sorry dear but I didn't want to rehash old scandals. People have forgotten about it."

Cindy jumped in, "but what if the thieves are committing the murders! We should go to the police with this."

"She's right Mildred," I said concerned. "You could be in danger."

Gloria was staring a hole in Mildred. She raised her hand and pointed at her. "Wait. You said jewels. I thought it was cash."

Mildred pressed her lips together and shook her head. "I shouldn't have let that slip. It was jewels. The police used money as a cover story hoping they would turn up at some point but they never did."

"If it was an inside job, then who did the police suspect?" I asked.

"The President of the bank."

"Well, let's look him up and ask him about it," said Cindy.

Mildred shook her head sadly, "We can't. Him and his wife were killed in a car accident about eight years ago."

"What?!" I asked, suddenly blindsided. "Do you mean William Wentworth?" The ladies looked at me like I was crazy. That's when I realized, they didn't know.

"William Wentworth is Bonnie's father." Now they all looked at me like I was a little crazy. "Bonnie used to be Lana Wentworth. Betty was her sister Hope. They were all involved in the car accident that killed my husband, Evan, and Travis's wife, Laura, ten years ago." My sudden declaration was met with silence.

Mildred finally spoke up, "Holly, I think you need to be a little more open with us from now on."

"I need to? You didn't know?" I had to take a moment to think. Who did know? Me, Vana and Lucy. Obviously Joe. Travis. Who else?

"Oh," said Cindy. "That's why you don't want to date Travis. That's so sad that you both lost your spouses in the same accident."

Her words of consolation hit me hard. I had never seen it that way. We had both lost our spouses. I was so hurt I didn't even think about how the news had affected him. "I'm such a heartless idiot," I muttered.

"Oh, no. We don't think that at all," said Cindy.

"Maybe a little blind," commented Maggs. At Cindy's glare, she hurriedly added, "You're very kind and thoughtful."

"Speaking of thoughtful," cut in Mildred. "Someone needs to take groceries to Betty. "I made extra keys to the Blume house." She held out a handful of shiny silver objects.

I rolled my eyes. "I've got to ask. Why can't we just drive up to Daria's house? Or why can't she go shopping in town?"

"Well." Mildred crossed one arm over her belly and used it to support her other arm and then rested her chin in her hand. We all watched her and waited. "I guess it really doesn't make sense to do it that way anymore. People will probably be more suspicious of us disappearing in there for hours."

"Ya think?" grumped Maggs.

"I suppose we could just be friends of Daria's," Mildred finally conceded.

"Thank you," I exclaimed. "I wasn't looking forward to traversing that tunnel by myself. Whatever happened to that cat?" We all looked blankly at each other.

"I suppose it must be at Daria's somewhere," said Mildred.

I STOPPED BY THE JAIL to see Bonnie, not knowing if they would let me in. Of course this was after sitting in the parking lot for half an hour waiting for Detective Moran to leave. Joanna said one of the guards owed her a favor and slipped me in.

Bonnie sat on the edge of the bed in the jail cell. A narrow window let in a sliver of daylight.

"What are you doing here," she sneered.

I just went for it. The less time I spent in her presence, the better. "I know the truth Bonnie. You've been looking for the money from the bank robbery 50 years ago. Is it because you've spent so much money stonewalling me that you're broke? Did you kill Paul?" I decided to forgo mentioning Louella and Pete until later.

Bonnie squinted at me. "Are you insane?"

"No. But I think you might be."

"That's a new low for you Holly. Accusing me of murder for money. I have all the money I will ever need. I don't need to steal it. Once again, you are coming to me with baseless accusations."

"I'm not the one who got arrested for murder," I retorted back.

Bonnie gave me one of her ghastly smiles that she didn't mean. "I'm innocent. That's why I'm going to go free," she said smugly. "Unlike you, I'm not guilty of any crimes."

Grr, I wanted to scream at her and slap that smug look off of her ugly face. "Once again Bonnie," I said through gritted teeth. "You killed my husband. NOT the other way around." I turned and left the office before I followed through on my desire. Just as I sat in the driver's seat my phone rang.

"Hello, Mildred."

"Holly, we need to meet right away at my shop. Can you get here quickly?"

"Of course I can. What's wrong?"

"It's Joanna. She's missing."

The door tinkled as I pushed through the door. Mildred was waiting for me and flipped the sign to closed as soon as I was in the candy shop. Maggs, Gloria and Cindy were sitting at a table waiting for me.

"What's going on?" I asked again.

"It's Joanna," said Maggs. "I went to talk to her to see if she had any new information and she hadn't shown up for work. The last time anyone heard from her was yesterday when she left the station."

"Aren't the police looking for her? I mean she is one of their own," I asked concerned. The ladies pursed their lips and looked at each other.

"It's just that moron Moran is in charge," said Gloria. "He couldn't find a bee if it stung his butt."

"What about Travis?" I asked.

"We can't reach him either," said Mildred. "His phone just goes to voicemail."

"This isn't like Joanna. I'm worried about her," said Maggs. "Why would someone take her?"

"What makes you think someone took her?" I asked.

"I went to her house and the door was open. She would never leave her door unlocked and her car wasn't there."

I blew out the breath I didn't know I was holding and held my face in my hands. "Just give me a minute to think."

"Do we have any way to locate her car or track her phone?" I questioned them.

Cindy raised her hand, "yes Cindy."

"Daria had a bunch of computers set up at her house, maybe she can help us."

"You were snooping in her house after she was so nice to us?" Gloria accused her.

Cindy shrugged her shoulders, "I might have accidentally opened the wrong door. Or multiple doors."

"What do you think Mildred? You know her better than us," I asked.

Mildred pressed her lips into a thin line, "Let me ask." She pulled out her phone. "Although I don't know how I'm going to explain this to her," she added as she glared at Cindy and then stepped away behind the counter to make her call. She came back a few moments later. "Daria said she'll call us back as soon as she has some information."

Well that was easier than expected. I didn't even ask how she was going to do this as I didn't want to know.

"We should all visit around town and see if anyone says anything about Joanna or her being missing," suggested Gloria. "Nobody ever suspects the blue haired ladies," and she fluffed her hair as she said it.

Despite the closed sign, we all looked up as the bell tinkled. Standing in the doorway was a man with short sandy hair. His face looked like he'd had a rough life but there was a glimmer of hope in his face as well.

"Excuse me. I'm looking for a woman named Meredith. I saw her picture in the paper taken during your Fall Festival." He held up a clipping from the local paper. Mildred took the clipping from him and looked at it, then passed it around to the rest of us. It was a picture from the children's booth upstairs, You could barely see Meredith in the background.

"Is she still here?"

There was pain and hope in his words. "Are you Colin Gray?" I asked. At the question his eyes brightened.

"Yes, I am. I'm her, I mean I was, her fiancee. Ten years ago there was a car accident and she disappeared and I never saw her again. I don't know what happened to her. I looked but I couldn't find her. Her name was never in the paper but I know she was in that car with her friends. I went and I asked Lana about her and she wouldn't tell me after a while I just lost all trace of her and I gave up but I saw her picture in the paper and I know it's her. I've got to find her. I love her and I still have her cat."

The rush of words tapered off and my heart went out to him. "I think we can help you get in touch with her. Are you staying in town?"

"Yes, I will, I'll get a room at the hotel. Thank you. Thank you. She's just the most thoughtful, considerate, loving person that I've ever met." His eyes started to water at the thought of seeing her again and I immediately knew how he felt. If only I could find my husband alive after all these years. I knew I had to do whatever I could to get those two back together again. "Here's my card. Text me and let me know where you're staying and we'll get in touch with you as soon as we have information."

He took the card from me and then suddenly hugged me. "Thank you. Thank you so much." Then he turned and left.

We all looked at each other in the silence that followed. "Guess you can get your Travis, that's not your boyfriend, back now," said Maggs.

Thankfully for Maggs, my phone rang. "This is Holly," I answered.

"Holly, this is Joanna. I just wanted to check on you and see how you were doing. You were pretty shaken up."

Joanna from the paper. My brain did its tingling thing again. I was missing something important. Then I had it.

"Holly, are you there?"

"Yes. I'm good, thank you. It's just that a friend is missing and I need to go find her." I clicked off and dialed Travis's number. The phone rang once and then clicked over to voicemail. I left a message because I hate when people just hang up.

"Travis, this is Holly. I think I may know where Joanna is. Call me back as soon as you get this message."

"Ladies. I think Meredith has Joanna." Hurriedly I explained about the two Joanna's. "Meredith asked how I knew about her history and I said Joanna told me. She took the wrong one."

"Maybe she has Travis too," said Gloria. "He's been hanging out with her an awful lot." I stared at her dumbfounded. "They may both be in trouble. Moran will never come help us. I think we're going to have to handle this ourselves," I said.

Mildred's phone rang. "It's Daria," she whispered, holding her hand over the receiver. "Hello Daria, did you find out anything?" She listened for a moment and then hung up. "She tracked Joanna's car to the Blume house."

That house again? Why could we never avoid it.

"Too bad the bear's not available," said Maggs. My reverie of imagining the bear getting to Meredith was interrupted by a cough from Gloria.

"Yes, right," I said and then we made our plans.

I PULLED MY CAR UP in front of Blume house. By this time, the sky was dark and stars were beginning to appear. The house sat in one big shadow. Gathering my courage I approached the front door and remembered I had returned the key. With nothing to lose, I tried the door knob, finding it was unlocked, I pushed it open slowly. Inside was dark, like really dark. Did I dare turn on my phone's flash? Then I remembered Mildred's words from the tunnel, to stay on the left so we wouldn't get lost. There was no furniture in the house so all I had to do was keep my hand on the wall and follow it around through the house until I found someone. A noise above my head made me jump. She must be upstairs.

Using my technique, although every part of me wanted to run outside, I followed the wall around the main entrance until I came to the left hallway and then walked straight across to the stairs. Knowing how they creak, I kept close to the wall and edged my way up slowly. Reaching the landing, I paused to listen which was difficult over the pounding of my heart in my ears. Why did I think sleuthing was fun?

This was terrifying. Creeping up the rest of the staircase, I paused at the top once again to listen.

Something brushed against my leg and I clamped my hands over my mouth to stifle a scream. Meow. It was a tiny, but comforting sound. It was just the cat. I let out a shaky breath. Its little paws made a soft thud thud as it ran down the hall and my gut told me to follow it.

Staying close to the wall I listened for the cat as it darted into a room. My eyes were suddenly blinded as the lights came on. And then they went out again as someone hit me from behind.

ANSWERS

When I came to, I was tied to a chair between Joanna and Travis. Meredith stood before me holding a gun. "The police are on their way, Meredith. They'll be here any minute."

She smiled at me. "No they aren't. I texted your friends from your phone. No one's coming." My heart sank at her words. I was so stupid. How many movies have I watched where this exact thing happens to the hero. Now we were all going to die because I didn't go to the police.

Maybe if I could stretch this out, one of us could get loose. "What happened to Pete, Meredith? Did he refuse to tell you where the jewels were?" Travis and Joanna both turned their heads to look at me.

Meredith pressed her lips together in a thin line and peered out the window.

"Who are you waiting for?" I asked. Bonnie was still in jail so it couldn't be her.

She turned back to me, her fists clenched at her side. "You know you wouldn't be here if you would have just kept your nose out of other people's business."

I shook my head sadly. "You didn't call the police because kids were causing trouble. You called them because they were interfering with your search. Is that what happened with Pete too? Did he refuse to tell you where the jewels were?"

"What do you know about it?"

"I don't think it's a coincidence that you live right next door to the house where the thief lived. The newspapers ran a cold case article about it a few years ago and you made the connection and discovered they were searching the building. I think you found out Pete was dating the teller during the robbery. That's why you came here. That all makes sense but why did you kill Paul?"

"Why do you think I did it? It was Bonnie's knife that was used."

"A knife that you planted."

She gloated at me. "You have no proof. You don't even have circumstantial evidence. Bonnie is the one that's going down for this."

I sighed. This wasn't going the way I planned. "Meredith, let's start again. What did Bonnie do to you?" Meredith clamped her mouth shut and then stared at her feet. "I know she did something to you and I think I know what it was."

Meredith raised her eyes to mine and I saw fear and anger mirrored in them. Bonnie told you that your boyfriend was in the car and died along with the cat. Let me tell you why that's not true. One, it was my husband that died and he would never have cheated on me. That's a fact. Two," I raised my fingers as I ticked off the reasons.

"You just left your boyfriend, there's no way he could possibly have gotten ahead of you and been coming from the opposite direction. Who told you that he was dead?"

The words barely left her mouth and I had to strain to hear them. "Bonnie told me."

"Did you know that your name was never mentioned in the paper? And there were no pictures of you. I think she did that too. Did Bonnie hate you for some reason?"

Meredith looked suspicious. "No. We were best friends until she killed Laura. She came to visit me in the hospital and told me she was protecting me by withholding my name from the press. She was so kind. The only other one alive was her sister and she was afraid of Bonnie."

I shook my head sadly before asking, "How did you find out she deliberately steered into that car?"

"I remembered!" She yelled angrily. "She deliberately killed Laura and my boyfriend and put my life at risk as well."

"But she didn't kill your boyfriend," I said quietly. "He's alive." I let the comment hang in the air.

"What?"

"Yes, he saw your picture from the Fall Festival and he contacted me. Did Bonnie have a reason to hate him?"

Meredith sagged to the floor as tears began to run down her cheeks. "What? He, he's alive? Ho, how?"

"Bonnie. That's why your name wasn't in the paper. She didn't want him to know. Why would that be?"

"You think you have it all figured out. You tell me," she sobbed.

"If she was that upset about Laura getting pregnant, then she certainly wouldn't have wanted you to get married."

"No she wouldn't."

"It's the funniest thing. Pete was wearing the wrong coat. That was the first mistake. Louella couldn't see without her glasses. She would never have gone hiking without them. That was the second mistake. You killed Pete in his house but when you were leaving, you must have seen Louella watching from the window, except that her grandchild ruined her glasses and she couldn't see a thing without them. But you didn't know that, did you?"

"I didn't find out until later," she admitted.

"You dropped her off early the day we went to the Blume house and then left and came back. You found her glasses in your car and threw them in the weeds. I know this is true because she left a voicemail and we heard the conversation." Okay, maybe that was stretching the truth but isn't that what all good detectives do?

"What I don't understand is why did you kill Paul? I know you did because Carol complained about getting left alone. You killed Paul and snuck out through the window but when the bear came through the front door, you couldn't get back in. That's why you were all out of breath when we saw you."

"I told you, I went to the restroom."

"I suppose Louella was an accident too?" I prodded her. That horrible feeling that I was missing something I should remember kept pushing in the back of my brain.

"Those jewels are here somewhere and I'm going to find them. One of them turned up in the pocket of the gang that was searching the old book club building. He found it in Pete's old house in Castlemeyer. That's how I knew Pete must have them but he wouldn't tell me where they were. He fell and hit his head. It was an accident."

"If that's true, then you haven't killed anyone. You could get away with just a minimum sentence," I said. "Maybe even community service."

She smiled. "Everyone knows this house is haunted. I'm just going to give the house some more bodies. You know I really liked you Holly."

"Meredith, you can't hope to get away with this. The police will find us and know it was murder and not the house." That's when the devil kicked me and got me into trouble. "If you're going to kill us, what are you waiting for?" That's when Joanna kicked me too.

"Travis did say you were too good at investigating. He was worried you would get yourself into trouble."Not if you die in the fire first." I gulped. She had me there. If she burned the house down, it would most likely be ruled an accident. After making sure my bonds were secure, she left the room. The three of us immediately began testing the ropes, trying to find a weakness.

"Travis, I've been such a fool. If we don't make it out of here I need you to know that I'm sorry. I'm sorry I've been so insensitive. You lost your wife too." Travis mumbled something through his gag but I couldn't decipher it. "Now that you won't be seeing Meredith anymore, perhaps I could make you dinner sometime to make up for the horrible way I've treated you. Well, obviously you can't answer me."

The floor suddenly shook. Joanna had been trying to tip her chair and the floor movement helped her and she crashed over onto her side.

"Joanna, are you all right?" She nodded her head and then proceeded to scootch up the back of the chair until she slipped her hands free. Just another mistake Meredith had made by just tying her arms behind and not to the chair. Then that sneaky little girl managed to get her hands under her bottom and pull her legs through her arms until they were in front of her. I was absolutely amazed.

It was at that moment that Meredith appeared in the doorway holding a gas can. "Stop that!" she yelled. The house shook again and the door suddenly swung shut in her face. We could hear the knob rattling as Meredith tried to open it. Meanwhile, Joanna, obviously ignoring Meredith's command, managed to free Travis, who in turn freed me.

A sudden series of thumps and bangs sounded in the hallway. Travis was the first to the doorway and opened it to see Gloria sitting on her butt on the floor holding the gas can up.

"Gloria?" I questioned.

"Go get her," she yelled at us. "Don't let her get away." Travis dashed down the stairs after her but he needn't have bothered. Halfway down the stairs, Meredith's foot slipped and she tumbled the rest of the way down landing at Maggs and Mildred's feet. Scott stepped into view and promptly arrested her.

"Did you see that?" I asked shocked.

"See that evil woman get what she deserved?" yelled Gloria as she triumphantly punched the air with her fist. "You betcha I did."

"No..." I couldn't finish. As I live and breathe, I know what I saw though. As Meredith ran down the stairs, the tread on one of the steps turned and she slipped. Travis had been right behind her and stepped on the same step and hadn't slipped. Gloria dashed down the steps behind him and I followed slowly, stopping at the questionable step. It was solid. I bent down and tried to move it with my hands. Nothing.

"What are you doing?" asked Maggs behind me.

"Nothing," I answered and went down the remaining steps to where Scott was reading Meredith her rights.

"You got the wrong Joanna," I said to her and then walked outside. Several more police cars and an ambulance were waiting on the drive. "Thank you ladies, you saved the day," I said as I hugged each one. "But how did you get here? Meredith said she texted you not to come?"

"I suspect the girls were listening in on the scanner," said Travis. "I was never interested in Meredith. Scott had his suspicions about her after the case in Castlemeyer. He's an undercover detective and so we arranged the date as a way to introduce the two of you without arousing her suspicion."

"That was so exciting," said Gloria.

Cindy looked glum. "I missed the whole thing."

"You should be glad that you did," I said, "it was terrifying."

"You did a wonderful job bringing the police," Mildred tried to console her.

"Uh oh," said Maggs. "Look who just showed up."

Detective Moran's car pulled into the drive and both he and Bonnie stepped out of the car. Bonnie was fairly gloating when she saw Meredith in handcuffs. Anger suddenly filled me and I planted myself in front of her.

"My husband never did have an affair. You slid that envelope under my door didn't you?"

Smugness filled her face. "A wife can never be 100 percent sure now, can she?" I wanted to smack that smugness off her face. The only thing that stopped me was the officer standing next to her with a gun and the fact she wasn't worth getting arrested over.

"Miss Holcraft, ladies, you can leave now. I'll expect you all to show up at the station tomorrow to have your statements taken," demanded Detective Moran.

I'm not gonna lie. His words got under my skin. We did all the legwork, saved everyone and he was going to step in at the last minute and take all the glory. I'll be darned if I was going to let him do that.That was when I got to watch someone else put both of them in their place.

"Bonnie Belmar, aka Lana Wentworth, I am placing you under arrest for the murders of Laura Wexler and Evan Holcraft. You have the right to remain silent." The rest of his words failed to acknowledge in my brain as I looked with wonder at my hero, Travis, as he handcuffed Bonnie.

"What are you doing? Who are these people? Miss Belmar would never..." Moran sputtered as Travis cut him off.

"Laura Wexler was my wife and Evan Holcraft was Holly's husband. Bonnie aka Lana Wentworth deliberately steered her car into Mr. Holcraft's vehicle in an attempt to kill Miss Wexler. That's murder in anyone's book."

Bonnie's face went white with shock. "Meredith told me everything," he added as he put Bonnie in the back of a police car. "

"William, you've got to help me," cried Bonnie to no avail as Detective Moran merely compressed his lips and watched as the car with her in it drove away.

"You can leave too," he snarled to Travis. "You've done enough." Travis nodded his head at Moran and walked away.

I watched as officers put Meredith into the back of a police car. I should be happy but I wasn't. Something didn't feel right. Meredith had been nothing but nice and polite to me. For her to suddenly act this way seemed out of character. I ran the thoughts of the last few minutes back through my brain.

I looked around at my friends who came to my rescue then I frowned. And suddenly I knew what was bothering me. I looked at Travis who was also watching Meredith. "Does Meredith strike you as a killer?"

He looked at me. "We suspected her of the robberies. She rented the house next to the old clubhouse and her fingerprints were all over the place.

"She never actually admitted to killing anyone. Carol said she asked Meredith to call me. She also said that Meredith was gone for 30 minutes but Meredith said Carol was gone forever. I just took Carol's word for it that Meredith was lying. But what if it was Carol that was lying?"

"Meredith was in the bathroom. I saw her go in and come out," said Det. Martin from behind us. "I was waiting with my girlfriend in the hall."

"Then she wouldn't have had time to kill Paul." I remembered how Bonnie had manipulated her and Joe. "She was in a psychiatric hospital for five years," I said, thinking out loud.

Travis looked at me. "How do you know that? There was nothing in her history."

I faced him bewildered. How could he not know? He was a police officer. "Meredith was the fourth person in the car that killed your wife."

"No, she never said..." his voice trailed off.

"I thought you said she told you everything?"

"I just said that to get Bonnie's goat. She didn't tell me anything." And just like that, the tickling in my brain came through loud and clear.

"She was trying to date everyone, she was looking for information. That's why she volunteered. She told me and I didn't get it. Pete. She was asking him about the jewels when he fell and died. Think about it, Louella, Pete and Mildred's houses were all broken into and they all worked at the bank where the jewels were stolen from."

"Then who moved Pete's body?" Gloria asked. Who indeed?

"Travis would you mind giving me a ride home, I'm just a little too traumatized to drive. I'll get my car later."

"Sure, no problem and if you give me your keys, I'll have someone drop your car off at your house."

"That would be great. Thank you."

Travis's car warmed quickly and I snuggled back into the seat. The headlights from his car cut through the darkness illuminating the pine trees and reflecting off the eyes of a stray animal. "Okay, spill it," he said. "I know you have questions to ask me."

Deciding to forgo the innocent look, I plunged ahead. "Did Meredith actually kidnap you and Joanna? I'm thinking not because I keep seeing you rub your head."

He turned and stared at me.

"Eyes on the road please."

"Sorry, I don't know. You're right, someone hit me on the back of the head and Joanna was chloroformed. Why?"

"I'm thinking there was someone else behind this. Meredith said she needed to find the jewels because she needed the money for medical bills. She certainly wouldn't have the funds to hire thieves to break into people's houses."

"She could have offered to split the money with them."

"True, but I'm sure they would have wanted a guarantee if the treasure was never found."

"True. So any idea who it could be?"

I shook my head. "I can't see any motive behind it. Except the jewels that may or may not exist."

We were both silent in the dark car, then Travis spoke. "Was she really in the car?" Seriously?

"It's just, Laura and I, we were having problems and maybe she could tell me what they were doing. I begged Laura not to go out with them but she said she had to. She called me that afternoon from Bonnie's and said she had news. Then she died. I found out at the autopsy that she was pregnant."

"I'm so sorry. And I'm sorry I've been so insensitive to your loss."

He gave me a quick smile. "It's okay. It's finally over now."

I smiled back. "Scott seems like a nice guy."

"He is." After that neither one of us had anything to say and it was a relief to pull up to my house and see Ginger poking her head through the curtains. "I guess someone's been waiting up for you."

Seeing her little doggy face peering through the window sent a warm feeling through my body. Dogs always love you. "Yes, she is," I said. "She's going to get a doggy treat too. Thanks for the ride Travis. I think you should talk to Meredith. That is if you can get past Moran. Get your answers so you can move on. I know I finally am." And I meant it. A feeling of relief swept over me like an ocean wave and left me feeling relaxed and calm. I got out of the car and then leaned back in.

"When you get back we have a drink and celebrate Bonnie going to jail."

"Sounds like a date," said Travis and his eyes twinkled as he put the car in reverse and backed out of the driveway, pausing in the street until I had gotten safely into the house.

"SO IT WASN'T BONNIE after all," said Lucy. Along with Vana, we were sitting around the bar at Tipsy's the next afternoon sipping a glass of wine and celebrating Bonnie's incarceration. The owner wasn't going to let us back in but we assured him that Shelby was out of town.

"No, but thanks to Meredith, she's going away for a long time. Too bad about Meredith though."

"You feel sorry for her?" exclaimed Vana.

"I think she was manipulated by someone but I can't figure out who. No one has a motive. If I could just figure that out." One name kept popping into my head but, once again the no motive thing had me flustered.

My phone kept buzzing in my jeans pocket so I pulled it out to find it was a call from Patty. What could she possibly want, the fall festival was a done deal. "I just need to take this, I'll be right back."

Walking out the door of the bar, I wished I had my jacket. It was freezing, frost crystals starting to appear on the car windows.

"Yes, Patty, what can I do for you?"

"We're having our follow up meeting for the fall festival tomorrow at the Blume house."

"Follow up meeting?"

"Yes. We do it after every event, go over what worked and what didn't and what we would do differently. It's especially important this year as we had issues and it was a new location. Is 2 pm good for you?"

"Do we have to go back to that house?" I asked as I hugged myself and began hopping to generate heat.

"Yes. It's important that we do it at the same location plus it helps us to remember what happened where, so we don't forget anything."

I blew out a breath. "Okay, but this is the last time I'm going to that house."

"Great, see you then." I dashed back inside to the warmth and then stopped and smiled at the sight before me. Great friends, laughing and having fun. Those are the important things in life.

I WOKE UP GRUMPY AND went through my day trying to find a reason to ditch the 'follow up' meeting at 2 pm eventually realizing that they would just reschedule it as I was the chairperson. "Ugh, what is up with that house?" Ginger looked up at me with her ears cocked and her head tilted as I spoke out loud. "I'm sorry Ginger. I just don't want to go." I dragged the last word out like a whiny child.

Finally, realizing I was going to accomplish nothing, I got in my car and drove to the Blume house. I was one of the first cars to arrive. Mildred and Patty were standing in the doorway waiting for me.

"Hello ladies. We might as well go in, we can sit on the kitchen counters," said Carol.

Mildred frowned. "Oh, I don't think she would like that."

I looked at her puzzled. "Who would like what?"

"Us sitting on the counters. It's not proper, you know." I looked back and forth between Patty and Mildred.

"What are you talking about?" Patty had the door unlocked and we all stepped inside. As usual the house was in pristine condition. I began walking around the front room confused. The three chairs from the room upstairs were now placed against the wall and the rope was coiled up on one of them.

"Is something wrong dear?" Mildred asked.

"Yes. Why is this house always so clean? And who is 'she'?"

Mildred and Patty exchanged a look. "The former owner of the house left it to her maid when she passed. Miss Dorothy Blume."

"Wait, the house isn't named after the person who built it? It's named after the maid?"

"Yes dear, that's what I said. Miss Dorothy Blume was a very fastidious woman. She fell in love with George Morecroft who lived up the hill. His parents looked down on Dorothy despite her now having a house and wealth. She's the one who had the tunnel built so they could visit each other. She called him her huggy bear."

Patty jumped into the story. "Some say they were secretly married but no one knows. Neither one of them ever had children and Dorothy passed away in this house."

Mildred picked up the tale. "Dorothy would never allow a speck of dust to stay in the home. She faithfully cleaned each room every day herself because 'no maid would ever do as good of a job.' And she still cleans it."

My face went through a series of manipulations as I went from disbelief to denial to belief and back again.

"Think about it dear. No one has ever cleaned this house yet, it always looks like this." Mildred waved her hand around the room.

"But what about the outside? It looks terrible."

Patty smiled. "Maids don't take care of the outside. That's for the gardeners."

"Sometimes things happen to people who don't respect the house," said Mildred.

My mind instantly shot back to Meredith falling down the stairs. "Meredith, she killed someone in here. I thought...I saw...something."

"It's best if you don't say anything. No one will believe you anyway," said Alma behind me, making me jump.

"Alma, could you make a little noise? You're going to give me a heart attack, sneaking up like that." I clasped my hand over my heart which was now beating rapidly.

"I'm sorry dear. Dorothy was my great, great aunt you know," she said fondly. "She used to throw wonderful parties." The rest of the ladies started filing through the door and we commenced with our meeting.

It was agreed that the issues this year, i.e. deaths, were a fluke and that outside of that, the house had been a wonderful venue. Poor Pete was probably turning over in his grave right now because we all decided to use this same venue for next year.

We also decided to have the house dedicated to Louella and would try to have the ice skating rink renamed in Pete's honor.

Alma stood to give the final remarks. "Ladies, you have all done a fabulous job at this event, despite the loss of Pete, it turned out remarkably well. I do hope that you will all volunteer for our next event which will be A Yuletide Christmas. We're going to be doing a tour of homes by snowmobile and sleigh." Everyone nodded and smiled and then Alma turned to me while I was still doing the smiling and nodding.

"Holly, you have really distinguished yourself this year, stepping up to be the chair for the fall festival. You're an excellent planner. How would you like to chair the Christmas event?"

"Oh, really, maybe one of the other volunteers would enjoy the opportunity?" I said hopefully but as I looked around, every single one of those women avoided eye contact with me. Before I could say another word Alma was already congratulating me.

"Awesome. Thank you. I know you will do a wonderful job." All of the other women started giving me congratulations and applauding. What could I do? I graciously accepted.

"If we're all done here, I promised my son I would bring him a batch of homemade cookies," said Carol as she walked to the door.

"Please give him our regards," said Patty. In an aside to me she added, "He just has never been the same since his father was killed in that bank robbery 50 years ago. I don't think he's ever going to move out of her house."

Carol turned with her hand on the doorknob. "I wouldn't talk Patty, your daughter just moved back in with her kids," she retorted, tossing her head back and turning the handle. The door didn't move. Frowning, she twisted it back and forth and then kicked it for good measure. *Nobody ever suspects the blue-haired ladies.* It suddenly all made sense.

"Carol, your husband was killed in a bank robbery?" Carol froze. "Is that why you killed Pete and Louella? Revenge? But why kill Paul?"

When she turned around her face was red with anger. "Meredith killed them and they deserved it. They planned that heist and got my husband killed!"

"But why Paul? What did he do?"

"He wanted the money. He heard about the break-ins and put two and two together. That money is blood money and anybody who wants it is just as guilty of killing my poor dear husband." Wow, and I thought Meredith was crazy. "Okay, but why stage Pete's body at the lake? Meredith said he fell and it was an accident."

Carol pressed her lips together. "That was Louella. Stupid woman. She didn't want people to think he died an old person's death by falling. She loved him too much for that."

"Why did you help her?"

Carol paused for a long time. "I was going to push her in. They could both die together but Meredith came along. Fortunately for me she did. I told her she was going to go to jail for moving a dead body and after that she just fell in line." She turned around and tried the door again but it wouldn't budge. Her shoulders sagged. "It's the house isn't it?" she asked in a small, tired voice. "I killed Paul and now it won't let me leave."

I was shocked at her callousness. She appeared to be the perfect housewife, an upstanding member of society. A small part of me felt sorry for her, knowing how difficult it had been to raise a child after the loss of my own husband. "I'm sorry Carol for what you had to go through but it doesn't excuse what you've done. I think you know that." She hung her head and sat down on one of the chairs. We all kept our distance from her just in case.

"Do you have to tell my son?"

"He's gonna find out," said Mildred. "You can't keep an adult away from television or the internet.

"Don't you worry none," added Gloria. "We'll make sure your son has everything he needs, even if he is 60."

"We'll visit you in jail and bring you cookies," said Cindy.

Tabitha just shook her head at us. "You all are a crazy bunch."

A DEEPER MYSTERY

Another successful murder mystery was done. Carol confessed everything to the police. I told Joe I would be back in a couple of days and then I took a trip across the country to the address Joanna had given me. The reporter Joanna, not to be confused with the receptionist Joanna.

The house I drove up to was a mini mansion, set back on a large lawn. Apparently the residents were doing well in their life. I parked by the curb and walked up the brick drive to the double front doors and rang the bell.

The door was opened by an elderly maid, dressed in a plain black dress and wearing a white apron, who looked down her nose at me which was quite a feat as she was the same height as myself. "Can I help you?"

"Yes, please tell the Wainwrights that I'm here to speak to them about a mutual acquaintance, William Wentworth? I'm pretty sure they will want to see me."

The maid gave a snort. "Wait here." She shut the door in my face and I waited. A few moments later she returned and gave a short, "follow me," and then walked away without waiting for me. I stepped inside and shut the door behind me. The entrance led through a tastefully elegant formal living room down the hall and into, what I imagined, was the family room.

Comfortable couches were set in front of a marble fireplace. Once again, it was tastefully decorated but I couldn't help but notice the lack of family photographs. A stunning elderly woman sat on the couch and an elderly gentleman, presumably Mr. Wainwright, leaned against the fireplace. We maintained silence until the maid left the room, closing the doors behind her.

"Hello, Mr. and Mrs. Wentworth." The woman looked frightened but Mr. Wentworth maintained his calm.

"I see you've met Joanna. She must have had a good reason to send you our way."

I walked over to the couch. "Do you mind?" I asked before sitting on the opposite side of Mrs. Wentworth. "You must be Julia. I can see the resemblance to Betty. I mean Hope." I gave a quick smile. "You might like to know that she took a cue from your book and her death was greatly overstated."

Julia looked relieved to hear the news but didn't say a word so I continued. "Joanna explained to me the circumstances of your disappearance and I understand. I've had my own run-ins with Bonnie, I mean Lana, myself. You also might like to know that she's been charged with the deaths of two people from the accident. That's not why I'm here though. Perhaps you could enlighten me on what happened with the theft of the jewels from the bank 50 years ago?"

Julia looked at William nervously. "Bill?" He crossed the room to sit by her side and hold her hand.

"I'll tell you what I know. Ten million dollars in raw uncut jewels were stolen from a safety deposit box in the bank. It belonged to a local jeweler. The police investigation concluded that it had to have been an inside job although no one was ever charged. There was never any evidence against anyone although the bank manager and a teller were suspected. They had the access but they also had alibis. Unfortunately, the security guard was killed as well. No one was ever caught. I, of course, was out of town at the time." He frowned at the memory.

"Mr. Wentworth, I think we all know you did it. What I specifically want to know is, what happened to the jewels? I don't want anyone else getting hurt over them."

He smiled at me as he nodded his head. "You are pretty savvy aren't you?"

"Well, I am a real estate agent. I deal with troublesome people all day long."

"Okay, well I'll tell you but if anyone asks, I'll deny it." He stood and began to pace back and forth in front of the fireplace. "My business was in dire straits, the bank was failing and I needed revenue. Uncut, untraceable jewels would have helped immensely. What I didn't count on was the backbone of a small community. When word got out about the theft, the community rallied around me. My business took off and in a short time I was extremely successful and didn't need that money anymore. I couldn't take the risk."

He paused in his story to look at his wife fondly and I sent a quick message on my phone. "We couldn't take the risk. Then after the accident, Lana was never the same. She became more angry and vengeful, if that's possible. Quite frankly, we were scared of her. Hope spent every moment with her, helping her. Then when we found the car tampered with, we knew what we had to do."

Bill stopped pacing and bit his lower lip. "I loved my daughters. The hardest thing I ever had to do was leave them, leave my little Hope behind." He abruptly cleared his throat. "What you want to know. The treasure's still out there. In Appleby. It's well hidden. I won't tell you where it is. I won't take the chance that something might implicate me after all these years. I won't."

I stood and slipped my purse over my shoulder. "Fair enough. Thank you."

Julia stood suddenly and grasped my hand. "Thank you. For the news about Hope." Tears filled her eyes. "If you wouldn't mind, perhaps you would let Hope know we're here. That was my greatest regret, leaving her with her sister, but I thought she might be safer if we were dead. Lana...she was always difficult...but after the accident, she changed. She became, I don't know, insane?" She hung her head and looked away. "Maybe she always was and I chose not to see it."

I hugged her. "I have something better for you," I whispered in her ear. Stepping back I turned to the door as it opened.

"Mom?" asked a timid voice. Julia rushed to the door and she and Betty fell into each other's arms. I took this as my cue to leave. Bill walked me to the door. "Thank you for that. I've missed her so much. You've brought us peace in our old age."

"You're welcome and don't worry about Joanna. She only told me so I could bring your daughter home."

I drove home happy that I could give Betty some peace in her life. How do you just abandon your child to a psychopath? I held no sympathy for her parents and if those jewels ever came to light, I would make sure the blame went squarely where it belonged.

WHAT'S NEXT FOR HOLLY?

I t's winter in Appleby and snow is on the ground. It's the perfect time for a quick jaunt to the beach where the weather is a balmy 75 degrees. Holly and the girls take a break from sunbathing to catch an open house at a million dollar listing. When a dead body appears and then disappears, it's up to Holly and the girls to find out who the murder victim is and why they were killed. Is the missing heir who was given up for adoption as a baby behind the murders? Was the mother poisoned?

The girls only have a few days to solve this mystery before the murderer gets away forever!

SIGN UP FOR MY NEWSLETTER at subscribepage.io/J9FVtd[1] and be the first to be notified when *Body at the Beach* is published. **You can check out all my books at MRDollschniederAuthor.com**

---

1. http://subscribepage.io/J9FVtd

ABOUT THE AUTHOR

M.R. Dollschnieder has over a decade in real estate and nearly 20 years writing for local newspapers. She lives in the California desert with her husband, two dogs, three cats and six chickens.

She spends her days in front of the computer writing while fending off the cats' attempts to assist her by sitting on the keyboard and standing in front of the monitors.

Don't miss out!

Visit the website below and you can sign up to receive emails whenever M R Dollschnieder publishes a new book. There's no charge and no obligation.

https://books2read.com/r/B-A-QLKLB-HBVZE

BOOKS 2 READ

Connecting independent readers to independent writers.

Did you love *Fear at the Fall Festival*? Then you should read *Bones in the Backyard* by M R Dollschnieder!

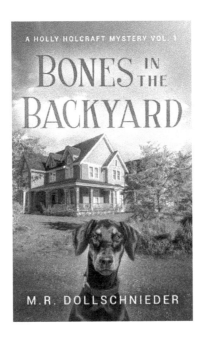

Hungry pigs. A missing ex. Can Holly find the truth before time runs out?

Real estate agent Holly's current transaction has been anything but easy. After numerous issues arise she has finally wrangled everything into order and escrow is about to close.

It all falls apart when her client calls in a panic: a dead body has been found in her husband's apartment and she is accused of his murder.

Can she figure out who killed Jerry before there's another victim? What secrets are her fellow agents hiding? Holly will be the first to say, she's no sleuth, but right now the town only has her and the bumbling hometown detective to set things straight. If she hopes to save her career and her client, she's going to have to step out of her comfort zone.

If you like *Hallmark Mysteries* and *Murder She Wrote*, then you will enjoy Holly's misadventures.

Milton Keynes UK
Ingram Content Group UK Ltd.
UKHW040256181024
449757UK00001B/74